13 Ways to Die

A Collection of Short Stories

Samantha Johnson

Copyright © 2020 Samantha Johnson

All rights reserved.

ISBN: 979-8-6545-0215-5

DEDICATION

For the Bee

CONTENTS

	Acknowledgments	i
1	Serpent King	1
2	Sapieha	6
3	Prodigal Son	10
4	Launch from the Moon	16
5	Emergency Exit	20
6	Playing Prey	28
7	Broken Circles	32
8	Visiting the Past	37
9	Toxic Poisoning	46
10	Tempering Joy	52
11	Summer Freezes	57
12	Vigilante	61
13	Release	65

ACKNOWLEDGMENTS

I would like to thank Devon King, Monica Zyla, Shauntelle Broeckert, Patricia Whiting, Martin Povey and Sandra Anderson who read one or more of these stories and provided valuable feedback. I'd like to thank my sister, Amber Spencer, for providing the inspiration for the character in Emergency Exit and Charlene Sapieha for allowing me to use her surname as inspiration. The first story, Serpent King, was a finalist in the 2018 Taxidermy Literary Contest and was published in the anthology *One Thing Was Certain: Which Do You Think It Was?* by Regulus Press.

1 SERPENT KING

"One thing was certain, that the white kitten had had nothing to do with it: - it was the black kitten's fault entirely. The Serpent King would not have found me if it had not been for the black kitten. I was lying on the edge of the river, my legs dangling over the bank, my feet cooling in the river water. My only companions were the kittens, we were alone together as we had been so many times before. I was unearthing within myself a pleasure that was all my own. A pleasure that would come of being wed to my own reflection in the water of that river. I, as you know, have steadfastly refused to marry any of the suitors my parents or brother have dragged forth."

I am sitting in a small, ornate chair across from my lady while she tells this story. The black kitten is currently sitting on the ledge of the single, small window, blocking what little natural light enters the circular room. The white kitten is not easily visible, camouflaged by a pillow, it's small body curled around upon itself. She gets up and walks over to each of the kittens in turn, petting them gently and murmuring words of comfort, to herself or them I am not certain. The black kitten pushes his head up into her hand, maximizing the effect of her attention. The white kitten makes a small noise and snuggles further into the pillow. The lamps, hung at regular intervals, burn weakly and casts long shadows, which continue to take on a life of their own. As she walks around the room, the shadows move with her and she interacts with them in a dance that is all her own.

"Indeed, my lady, the ceremony will take place tomorrow. Your father has commanded it."

"I am no longer his to command. His reign is finished, it will not last the day."

"That is treason, my lady."

"It is truth, no less."

"This kingdom lives faithfully by the scriptures; it will last a long while yet."

She gives a wild, bitter laugh, the shadows arching high, becoming a heckling crowd. "Ah yes, the bastardized version that is preached to us. I have read the stone, seen it with my own eyes."

"The stone is lost, nobody has seen it for many generations."

"The stone is a short distance away down the forbidden path."

"The forbidden path? No…no, no, my lady."

She waves me off, returns to her seat. The shadows fall to the floor, huddling around her. The white kitten wakes up, stretches and yawns, jumps down off the bed and comes padding over, gracefully leaping onto her lap and curling itself back into a ball, instantly asleep again. The black kitten turns, small black eyes glowing, and hisses.

"It will be soon now," she says.

She lays her head back against the chair, closing her eyes and idly caressing the white kitten. "We have jumped too far ahead, you understand nothing."

"My lady, I am here to understand."

"You are a spy, nothing more. I will tell you my tale, it will come to life for you. I wonder, will you survive the ordeal?" She opens one eye and glares at me, then shuts it, her dainty mouth curving into a small smile.

"Where was I?"

"The edge of the river my lady."

"Yes. The white kitten was beside me, always the more dependent of the two. Gifts from my sisters, the balance of light and dark, an equalizing force." That bitter laugh again, then: "More than they know. The black kitten was off cavorting around, brewing up mischief. I had learned to let him be, he always returned on time and appeared to be immune to danger."

"That sounds like neglect, my lady."

"I am not their keeper, they are mine. We have been going to the riverbank since they were weeks old, I had my preparations to do for the ceremony."

"Is that what you were doing on the day in question?"

"No, you are not listening. I was enjoying the moment, the feel of my body on the sand, the sun on my skin. I had removed my outer layers and was lying only in my shift, which was pulled up past my knees, my arms spread wide, my fingers tracing patterns in the sand."

"My lady, if you had been seen."

Her head jerks up, eyes stormy. The white kitten gives a small hiss in protest, the black kitten turns his back to look out the window again. The shadows start swirling around her chair, I lift my feet to avoid contact with them. "If you insist on interrupting me, I will not continue."

"I beg your pardon, my lady. I will refrain until the end."

She rests her head back, the shadows calming as she does so. "I heard the familiar sound of the black kitten racing through the underbrush along the path leading to the river. His small paws hit the gravel at the edge of the beach, causing them to rattle and collide, then he was beside me on the warm sand. He curled up by my ear as he always does, his purr thundering through his small body and reverberating through mine. It is a most comforting sensation." She lifts her legs, "footstool." The shadows obey, pushing the small stool over from the bed until it is below her feet. "Massage."

One shadow detaches itself from the others and circles around her legs and feet, kneading them as she makes small sounds of pleasure. I turn my head away, embarrassed by the intimacy of the moment.

"You always were squeamish, get ready for your skin to crawl." Her voice has softened, a sultry quality now tinges the edges of her words, causing prickles on the back of my neck and a bead of sweat to form, trickling down the inside of my shirt.

"I am the court scribe, I have heard all manner of misdemeanors in my time."

"Really? We shall see."

"I am confident, my lady."

She makes a snort of derision, continues with her tale: "The black kitten had not returned alone, I did not hear the approach of the other, only felt the pressure on my skin, then the weight of him on my body. I was consumed my him, his length enveloping me before I had time to react. He explored every inch of me, and I lay still, I knew better than to fight such a force. I kept my eyes closed, believing the sight of him would cause fear to roil in my stomach, induce me to lash out in a stupid act of self-preservation. He slithered off me and I thought he was gone, until I felt his tongue, flicking along each part of me, until I had been fully tasted and tested. I admit I moaned in pleasure at times, I had never been touched in such a way."

I swallowed, my throat dry, my pen hovering over the scroll, a dead instrument. I shook my head to clear my thoughts but the image she painted was vivid. I admonished myself, I needed to regain control, remember my station in life. She picked up the white kitten and gently placed him on the floor, stood up and walked behind my chair.

"Oh, you've made an error, your scroll is quite a mess. Looks like you will need to start again." She bends down, her lips right against my ear, "unless you want to ravish me now?"

"No…no, my lady… I am well, let us continue…*please*."

She stands up, laughing at me, and walks over to the bed while I fumble with my quills, dropping the scroll and knocking over the ink bottle. She lies down on the bed, stretching her body luxuriously. I stop and watch her, forgetting every rule that has been hammered into my feeble skull since I was a child.

"I believe I have unsettled you."

She does not look at me but lies on the bed and allows her hands to roam over her body. I am entranced, forgetting my scroll, the ink spreading a path across the floor, staining my shoe. I stand and take a step towards her. Both kittens race towards me, their little fangs bared, the shadows rising behind them, an immovable barrier.

"I belong to the Serpent King." Her hands circle her abdomen and pause there, "I now carry his child and it is death for another to desire me. I have gone to him every night for the past two months and he has done things to me that others could never imagine." She rolls over onto her front, rests her head on her hands, looks over at me and winks. "Do you know he can alter shape and take on a human form? When he does this, his eyes are emeralds, his body glitters in sunlight and glows by moonlight. His snake-skin pattern stretches into a faint tattoo that can be traced in a continuous pattern around his body. He has bed me in all his forms, I am his gift and his life. He will have me, and I will bear his heir. This kingdom is finished, it has denied him his rightful place, it has rewritten the scriptures and devoured itself on power and greed."

A shadow rears up in front of me, extending a limb and pushes me back in my seat, where I sprawl over the edge. Another shadow races around my legs, strapping them to the chair and a third takes my arms behind me. I am unable to right myself and sit there, bolted and tilted, a puppet on a string.

She sits up on the bed, her hands ripping her bodice apart, shredding the sleeves of her dress. Standing, she starts to walk the room again, the kittens following.

"You will all feel his wrath now. My pious father with his petty quarrels and fat incompetence. My mother, the wench, who perhaps should have come clean about the true nature of my parentage. Let us not forget my brother, with incestuous designs on all his sisters. He has not been able to touch me, not in my supposed virgin state. The only reason, I would wager, he is so determined to see me marry. The weak husbands of my darling sisters turning a blind eye each time he beds them."

My head is at an odd angle, a crick forming in my neck, but I must respond to her, attempt to divert the disaster she is courting.

"It is tradition, my lady, as written in the scriptures."

"Lies and treachery. You forget, I have read the original. They preach us nothing but a glorified misinterpretation of the truth." She is continuing to work at her dress, shredding it apart so that it falls around her in tatters. "So now we come to it, my incarceration in this tower. Who found out about my nightly visits to the Serpent King? Three days and nights I have been here. Who betrayed me? Who is responsible?"

I make a small noise in the back of my throat and she waves her arm in a circle. The shadows release me, and I tumble onto the ground along with the chair.

"Is it a betrayal?" She is muttering to herself now, pacing back and forth in front of the window. My legs have gone numb from the pressure of the shadow and I struggle to sit upright. Before I can make the effort to stand, she rushes over to me, kneels so her face is level with mine and I am looking into her blazing, green eyes.

"Which one, dear scribe? A betrayal or conspiracy? Are they planning to allow me my marriage to my reflection tomorrow or are they going to make me a sacrifice? Which do you think it was that led me up here, will lead you all to your deaths?"

With that I hear the first whistle and roar, the ground shakes and the entire castle shifts and moves. She stands up and crosses over to the window, throwing back her head and laughing with a manic glee. I scramble to my feet and stumble over to see, the tingling sensation along my legs causing me to walk with a lurching gait. I peer out the window and see a man, his skin glittering in the sun, his emerald eyes burning bright. The walls around the castle are covered in snakes, a swirling mass of them, smothering guards and pulling them over the edge, where they fall to the ground. The guards remain lifeless while the snakes return to climb the wall again. Another whistle and roar, a larger impact, I hold the ledge to keep my balance.

"Time to run, little scribe," her lips barely move, the words coming out of her mouth in a hiss.

I start to back up and she pursues me, her face a mask of rage and hatred, her words chasing me, "which do you think it was scribe, *betrayal* or *conspiracy*?"

I turn and bolt for the door, taking one last look before I wrench it open and collapse into the hallway, her voice thundering this final question after me. I crawl down the hallway before staggering to my feet and running. I have trouble focusing on where I am going, my vision transfixed by the image of her standing in the middle of the room, her dress in disarray, the shadows spinning circles around her. The kittens flanking her on either side, their small bodies arched, the hair on their backs standing straight up, their small faces contorted into hisses. Her question echoes in the chaos of a building being torn asunder.

Which do you think it was? Which do you think it was? Which do you think it was?

2 SAPIEHA

Some young thing hung wind chimes on the tree near my headstone, which is old and crumbling. My grave sits in the far corner of the cemetery, in what was once a prominent position. Wars, famine, and epidemic caused the expanse of the area to be truncated, the land sold off for other, more profitable ventures. Mass graves were dug for the thousands of corpses when occupation and quarantine caused havoc. Bodies were thrown unrecognizable into the street to be collected by wraiths when no living relatives remained to make amends.

I dreamed of death for so long it will be a struggle to focus on life. Not a young death nor a small one, but the everlasting kind in a solid wooden box, the lid heavy with velvet, which quickly became a purple lined trimming for rodent burrows. The knife wound of disregarded memories begin to pierce through me and lacerate again and again while I struggle against them.

A body arousing lust wherever I made an entrance withered to powder long ago, my bones now dry and dusty, decaying within this enclosed space. My tortured soul is not healed by this slumber, it probes the soft spot of my elapsed regrets and flashes them back to me. I turned away too long, and the soft, musical notes woke me. Groggy but growing stronger, I will rise back up into the world to come and get you. I will find you and bring you home.

My name is the Baroness Zelda Sapieha, born a princess of low rank and married to the Baron Sapieha at the tender age of fifteen. There was a time when my name and rank would have been sung aloud by others, my entrance heralded as an event. This centuries-long death has forced me into the unenviable position of performing my own introductions. Reduced to poverty, with rank and title stripped, the family name no longer holds sway the way it used to.

Within days of arousing, a storm crawls across the landscape. I whip myself into a frenzy and call it toward me, howling with it as I go screaming through town. My reward is doors closed tight, curtains and blinds slammed shut, the streets barren and empty. No welcoming stranger allows me comfort out of the elements.

I am left to blow around the streets, whistling her name while the foolish girl does not answer. Everyone vacates the cobblestone laneways, locking themselves away as they did at the end of my life. Abandoned and alone in our huge house with bedrooms sealed off to hide the stench and decay of all I held dear, everything left to die and rot in isolation.

Depleted, I return to my grave to wait as the storm moves off. This once beautiful and well-cared for cemetery is in disarray. The nearby river cuts a wider path than in my day, while the land speaks of recent flooding. Exploring in search of recognizable names, I find headstones disintegrating or toppled over with broken pieces scattered in all directions. The ground is uneven with tree roots rising above it, a hazard of a place to those confined to flesh and blood.

Rodents have gone wild, digging around the grave markers and tunneling underneath coffins. Most of the tombstones are unreadable with the engravings eroded away. My task becomes a wasteland of disappointment. Anger is what I wish for, a fury against all I see as unreasonable. Resignation is my sole reward, along with a deep aching need. I yearn to hide away once again, to descend back into blissful blackness.

The chimes momentarily silent, I curl myself into the cave of bracken partially covering my headstone and slip into a brooding meditation. Months later, she finally arrives. The first time I see her, she is bending down to peer into my hollow of abundant blackberry. Upon reading the name - one of the few still legible in this disregarded and neglected place - she sits heavily on the moist ground. Tears flood her cheeks with rainbow hues and her face holds a distant, dreamy expression. She visits daily over the next few weeks: clearing away the bracken, bringing flowers, planting a rose bush, and removing the cursed chimes. Without them, I could slip back into the unknown. Fighting one desire with another, I persist above ground to fulfil my final duty.

My husband's sister was a flighty, uncontrollable enchantment with an allure so strong she could be tolerated, although not always enjoyed. Sitting beside me, she would squirm and bounce like a young child, never able to keep still. Her attention could not be maintained on a single thing, her conversation a hummingbird in flight. Loved by many and adored by a few, they would follow her around, playing the childish games she favoured. A string of lovers remained loyal until the day she died, sitting by her bedside while she was lost to a mysterious ailment that drained the life out of her in a few months.

This one, a mirror image of myself in appearance, reminds me of my sister-in-law in mannerisms, the way she tilts her head, the quick movements she makes. Although, it must be said, she spends too much time alone, wandering here and there, immersed in a world no other can visit nor understand. Never patient, I am irked I do not know her name because she always arrives alone, and none have spoken it.

As she reclines against my headstone, I hover above to weave a web of memories, eventually bringing my spirit self near her face. If I get too close, she will bring both hands up and rub with a fierce energy. My aim is achieved when she opens her green eyes, allowing me to investigate them and delve deep into the past through her.

The despair and joy of generations is apparent, she is a link between my time and hers. I want to kiss her and pass on the wisdom I acquired during my lifetime and the greater knowledge achieved through death. It is not permitted; the land of the dead must remain separate from the living and I am forced to simply observe, grinding my disappointment into a churning hope.

After attending to my grave and surrounding area for so many weeks, there comes a day when she does not appear, followed by several more. A restless energy overtakes me, and I thrash around the cemetery, not willing to leave should I miss her if she shows up. After days of waiting, she finally arrives carrying flowers and a vase, placing them carefully on my grave marker. I am instantly calm until she does not settle down on the ground but turns immediately to leave.

On impulse, I accompany her, wanting to discover what has replaced her daily visits. Following behind while she rides a two-wheeled contraption, I ascend on a light breeze and remember the feel of life in my hair. I am hoping she is off to meet a lover, but her destination is only my old house. Inside the fog of death, I'd forgotten how to reach it and instantly regret my long absence.

Once I see it, the flood of memories is overpowering. It has altered in the centuries since I lived there, but I can see the original structure within. I focus on my girl to abate the sensations of remembrance and feel a little hope for her when, after waiting longer than is acceptable, a young man approaches. He looks promising from afar, tall and slender with white blond hair; however, as the figure advances it becomes clear he is merely a gardener.

Here is a man whom women will swoon over, despite his lowly position. One who, if he so wishes, could have them eating out of his hands, those soiled with the evidence of his toils. When he speaks, his voice is low and melodious, musical and heartbreaking at the same time. "Nice to see you again, Cassandra."

A name for her at last. Such a good name despite the superstitions of those too ignorant to understand. Alive, I would sink my teeth into it, savour the feel of it gliding around inside my mouth. Dead, I allow excitement to bubble inside me as I race around the grounds, causing hats to blow off other, less interesting, visitors. I return to Cassandra and the gardener several times, but their corporeal bodies move too slow for my liking.

Unable to contain my impatience, I leave them to their rambling and venture inside to explore the house. First stop is my chambers, where I get caught in the doorway and find myself unable to enter. It has altered beyond recognition, the arrangement and selection of furniture unfamiliar to me. A family of four walk down the hallway, their earthly energy giving me the push required to move past the invisible boundary.

I ensconce myself in the bay window, which is cushioned with large, thick pillows. Engrossed in the view, I tune out all behind me to enjoy, once again, the panoramic aspect of the front lawns and the sunshine sparkling off the river in the distance. Lingering there, I barely notice the shadows lengthening as the sun arcs across the sky.

The furniture is cordoned off, none may touch it. The house feels unlived in, a monument to times past. There is a moment where a young girl - probably not more than five years old - comes rushing over and stares at me, pointing me out to her parents. They tell her they see nothing while the child demands they look closer. She continues to gaze over her father's shoulder, waving as she is carried away. I wonder what she saw, how I presented myself to her young eyes but quickly lose interest as the family moves out of sight.

Absorbed in memories of home, I almost miss the moment Cassandra walks towards the entrance, the tall youth by her side. At the gate, he leaves her after a short and decidedly unromantic farewell. Cassandra picks up her two-wheeler, which, I realized on our way here, is one of the quieter forms of transportation available. Horses seem to be in short supply, fast moving metal boxes taking their place.

Perhaps I should go with her, go back to what others determined to be my final resting place. I am unable to do it, the world outside has become a chaotic stream of noise and confusion since I lived. Unwilling to remove myself from the window seat, I choose to stay behind to enjoy the relative quiet of what was once my residence. Turning away from her departing figure, it occurs to me that having called her to me, it is she who brought me home.

3 PRODIGAL SON

An over-powering, putrid stench wakes me. Dry heaving my way off the bed, I wrench a window open, pressing my lips against the dirty screen to inhale exhaust fumes, a welcome alternative. Holding my breath, I race out of my tiny bedroom and through the living room. Stumbling on the detritus littering the floor, I manage to make it across and open the patio doors.

I step outside and wait for the worst of the odour to dissipate. My solution yesterday, when the smell wasn't quite so over-powering, was to repeatedly slam my fist into the ill-fitting lid of my garbage can. Not surprisingly, it didn't work, and my too small garbage can, the sole one in my apartment, was unable to contain whatever rots within.

Already late, I don't have time for this shit. Taking short gasping breaths, I race back inside to the kitchen and haul the bag out of the can. A steady flow of fluid drips from the bottom and I drop it back in. My fist hammers the lid again, which now resembles a concave mouth rather than a seal. The entire thing will have to go. I spot a heavy-duty plastic bag and pounce on it. It contains the dirty laundry which, inconsiderate leech I am, was going to be left at my parent's house for my Mom to do. This is what I've come to, asking the broken to do my housekeeping because I'm too lazy to do it myself.

Dumping the laundry on the floor, I open the bag wide and tenderly lift the can. The bag easily dwarfs the inadequate container, and I wrap the extra plastic around it, grab some duct tape and seal the smell inside. Dumping the package by my front door, I decide the clothes I'm wearing will have to do and the post-alcohol fumes emanating off my body benevolently ignored by my immediate family. My only saving grace right now is there are no girls with unknown names in my bed or friends sleeping on the couch.

Another fifteen minutes are wasted searching for my phone before locating it in my back pocket, a crusty coating causing it to stick slightly to the inside lining. Hauling it out, bits of blue fabric adhere to the mystery substance. I pick at it with my nail, trying to figure out what it is and how it got there. My screen lights up showing me three unwanted phone calls from my less than adoring father and I reluctantly dial voicemail.

The tirade begins with, "how could you do this to your mother?" All messages are deleted before the first one completes itself, a small victory on my part.

Hopping down the hallway toward the elevators, I have the bag in one hand and am pulling on shoes with the other. Stopping at the garbage chute, I attempt to shove the load in, but it gets jammed. There is the moment before, fist punching sides and top of bag, and the moment where I reach around and open my hand, the one clutching my keys. A split second of stillness ensues as I listen to the slide of metal on metal, a soft clunk as they hit bottom.

The bag remains where it is, causing the stale air of lonely lives, a distinctive attribute of the building I reside in, to be replaced by decay. Adrenaline coursing through me, I take the stairs three at a time. Two flights down the old skills return and my butt hits the railing, one landing after another sliding past, wanting to be as low to the ground as possible before I take a ride in the garbage chute after my keys.

On the ground floor, old Mrs. Wilkens, who gives me cookies occasionally, stands in wide-eyed horror as I wiggle myself into the chute. A bag from above clunks me on the head when I'm halfway in before my centre of gravity shifts, and I go sliding down, my tailbone taking the brunt of a hard landing at the bottom. Clawing my way to standing through a small mountain of bags, I spot the glitter of keys and dive as the compactor clicks on.

It is a miniscule triumph, keys back in hand as everything on the other side of the metal jaws is crunched to flattened grime. There is no return, the chute angled steeply to ensure all garbage, your truly included, makes it into the compactor mouth. The pull at my feet lures me toward an undignified death while a crack of light to the side gives hope and, desperate, I deliver repeated kicks to the panel. One, two, three and it swings open. Oh, sweet relief of freedom. I scramble out and tumble to the ground, jarring my already bruised tailbone.

A dump urchin now, competing for the title of world's biggest slob, I rise shakily to my feet. Bits of garbage are stuck to my hair and clothing and, even without a mirror, I know I'm classy as all get out. Fuck it. I hop in my shit box car and, predictably, it won't start. How it got here last night from the bar, who knows, but it's not leaving. I storm around the back of the concrete monolith I call home to the gated, never locked storage area and grab my bike. Peddling furiously, I cross through traffic, racing in and out of cars on a daredevil mission. Horns honk, and assholes lean out windows to curse as I sail past, my head pounding and eyes streaming.

It's not the kind of late where you rush in and there are smiles all around along with gentle greetings along the lines of, ah, there's Liam, good to see you. No, this is the type of late that is embarrassing for everyone involved. Dad shakes his head as I come through the door, disappointed beyond speech. Mom's in tears again, doesn't appear to have stopped since I saw her two days ago. All decked out in a dark suit is my kid brother with a pretty, blond girl beside him in a knee-length, black dress that swirls around her thin legs.

"Hey, Jimmy."

"James." He's got a hard stare, all macho and mature, eyes roving up and down my decrepit person.

"Oh, right. Got it." I peer at the girl, my neck stuck out long, a sloth inspecting an unfamiliar being, "I'm Liam."

He pulls her into him, a proprietary hug, protection from his older brother, "my girlfriend, Amelia." She produces a shy smile, ducks her head back against Jimmy's shoulder. Sorry, James now.

Trying to be jocular, ignoring the slight, "girlfriend at fifteen, good on you." I swing my arm around to chuck him on the shoulder, but he moves away, avoiding contact. Catching sight of my hands, I wince at the green stains on the palms and blackened fingernails wiggling for contact.

"Sixteen…four months ago."

Right, the birthday I missed, failed to attend, bunked off. The day he got the car he'd been saving for years to buy. Jealousy is what happened, envy at my kid brother ten years my junior. Couldn't face it so I went out and partied, got so hammered I lost three days, almost lost my job. No worries, I tell everyone, I'm still hanging on. I don't mention it's by a single fingernail, no point in giving all the details up front.

My Dad ushers me off to the shower, where a new set of clothes hangs behind the door. Underwear and socks sit tidily on the counter, and a pair of polished black shoes are arranged neatly on the floor. Behold the bounty of my parent's generosity.

In the car, on the way to our destination, the only sound is my mother's weeping. Nobody speaks. James holds Amelia tight against him, keeping her as far from me as possible. As we head inside, there is a distinctive distance between me and the rest of my immediate family, me hanging back, reluctant to enter through the double doors and partake in what lies ahead. Halfway through the service, I bail, sneaking out when nobody's watching. Phone in hand, I'm texting as I walk down the road and Ramone is the first to respond.

Within minutes, he drives up, arriving in his drug money Mustang with the music blaring and Twitch semi-conscious in the backseat. Window rolled down, he gives me an appraising glance, "Liam, look at you all dressed up."

Shrugging off the comment, I pull the jacket off and tug open the passenger door, sinking into the leather seat, my pressed white shirt pulling up at the back. The seat cushions my bruised tailbone and, even though the temperature has hit double digits, I punch on the heated seat for a spot of therapy. Ramone bobs his head, waiting for my seatbelt to click into place. A man who snubs his nose at law enforcement in every other way won't drive away until everyone in his car is safely buckled in.

Satisfied, he gives the command, "let's go do some crime boys."

A sentence causing Twitch to come alive, his head doing a familiar dance on his shoulders, his arms jerking arrhythmically. Once he starts moving, nothing stops, his entire body a contradiction, all going in different directions.

With a voice, cracked and underused, he manages to squeak out, "what about Jib?"

"Yeah, didn't forget."

Ramone drives around the houses, checking for action, trying to spot unforeseen opportunities. Twitch gets worse the longer it takes us to get to Jib. Ramone whips his head around when the backseat convulsions become too distracting, "it's cool, he's gonna be there forever. Walk-in clinics are never fast."

Everything halts as we drive by student residence. In our buzzed up, half-stoned state it's too good to be true. A pudgy guy is laying out a blanket on the miniscule lawn, decked out in a speedo with white, flabby skin bared for all to see. We drive around the block a half dozen times so we can pass him repeatedly with our heads out the window while yelling obscenities, wolf whistling and causing traffic to slow to a crawl. Disappointingly, the guy's eyes remain stubbornly closed as he absorbs our abuse along with the UV rays.

On the last pass, Twitch puts his head out the sunroof, standing full height, arms flailing. His stunt catches the attention of a cruiser going in the opposite direction. Cop must be on his way for donuts because he doesn't stop or jump the meridian to come after us. Only does a lazy flash of his red and blues and half a hairy arm appears out the window with palm facing down. Sit, Twitch, sit. Good boy.

We lope into the doctor's office to collect Jib as some fat fuck is talking to the receptionist. We take over a row of chairs, legs out long, arms crossed over chests, sunglasses resting on the bridge of our noses. Twitch looks to be having a seizure, but the spasms abate when I hard elbow him in the ribs.

Fat guy, with his high-pitched voice, needs another appointment, a form faxed to AISH and wants to explain the details of today's visit to the bored and uninterested receptionist. "He told me to stop eating late at night," a half-hearted wheezing chortle he lacks the energy to finish is emitted, "which is what my family said."

Trying not to laugh, we stifle our sniggers behind hands and clenched teeth. This is the mutants we are, infants in grown bodies, still getting a kick out of being mean and razzing those less fortunate.

Fat guy half chuckles while turning his weight to the door, side-stepping awkwardly, "see you next time."

I make the mistake of catching Ramone's eye and we explode, our full-blown snorts and hoots echoing off the walls. The guy lumbers off unhearing, forging off the violence of life by packing in its' insults. Minutes later, Jib saunters out, proudly clutching a fist-full of prescriptions.

"Scored boys," he says, waving the papers in our faces.

The pharmacy in Safeway is the grateful recipient of Jib's prescriptions. While waiting, we skulk up and down the aisles, leaving partially empty bags of chips, open boxes of cookies, and a few drained colas in our wake. A grocery clerk starts following, so we line up at Starbucks and place an order. Flirting aggressively with the young barista, we make her blush over and over while leaning against the counter enjoying our power.

Jib's name is called over the speakers and he races to the back, almost taking down an old guy with wispy white hair who is pushing a walker. It earns him a sharp rebuke from a puff of an old woman, her shrill voice ringing down the aisle as he rounds the corner. We're doubled over, latte foam spewing from our lips and noses, every other customer giving us a wide berth. Back in the car, pill popping ensues, greedily inhaling pills from each bottle in Jib's small paper bag.

Ramone decides we are ready for action and drives to a house he wants to hit. Guy who lives there, so Ramone informs us, is a self-important shit who needs to fall from his ivory tower of superiority. We cruise the neighbourhood, windows down on the car, music low. Each house on the block is examined for potential trouble, looking for anyone outside working in their yards or nosy parkers peeking out behind the tremble of a curtain.

Satisfied, we pull into the back alley and park behind the designated house. It's decided, since I'm the smallest, I'll go first. Gate is bolted and locked, but the fence, six feet of solid wood, is easy to scale even in my new clothes. I'm up and over, the last hit from a needle helping me realize the full scale of my invincibility.

Not a half-hour later, I'm being loaded into an ambulance, one eye puffed to closing, paramedics throwing questions at me. My breathing is fine, no allergies, but I'm having trouble talking. One or two of the bees must have climbed in my gaping maw as I let loose an unholy howl. The wail continued as I burst through the unlocked front gate, a cheerful sign warning of bees on the premises tumbling off the nail and clattering to the ground.

The swarm gave up after a few blocks, but I kept running for six more. At a stop sign sat an idling bright orange SUV and I collapsed on the hood. The driver, diverted by my arrival from his phone, stared in horror. When he jumped out, I thought for an instant he was an inside out leprechaun. The guy was so tiny, I thought I was hallucinating. His outfit was nothing less than garish, black swirling designs on green tights worn underneath red shorts with a matching extra-large t-shirt.

Out of air, my muscles protested further exertion and down I went, my new clothes tattered and stained. It's not surprising my twin sister, the one we placed in her eternal resting place today, hasn't spoken to me in over three years. Joke's on her though, her eco-tourism and good deeds leading her into the path of an insect that snuffed her life out while I'm still breathing, living the good life. My final insult to the day and her memory is to say nothing, only nod my head yes, when the paramedic asks if the address on my licence is correct. My parents are going to freak when the bill comes.

4 LAUNCH FROM THE MOON

The moon is where I am, on the moon. In my humble opinion, I should not be on the moon; however, NASA deemed it worthy to send me here, yet again. I am off on my own, riding full tilt in one of the moon buggies, a reckless display of independent rebellion. To assure my freedom, I've disconnected the communication device inside my helmet, a little trick I perfected on my last mission.

Yes, the previous trip was to be the final trial before the launch to Mars. Not being forced to communicate, clicking on and off my device, would have been a huge advantage during the five years of travel, not to mention afterwards. I mean, come on, it's a long time to spend cooped up with a small group of people. Sure, we all know each other, but there is a huge difference between sticking it out for a week or two compared to years of suffering someone else's company in a confined space.

Once the ship for Mars launched, there was next to nothing that was going to call it back to Earth. Nope, it was a do or die mission and NASA, in their infinite wisdom, chose to terminate it before anything happened. They proclaim it is only postponed. Yeah, like indefinitely. Now, here we are back on the moon again, conducting the same old experiments and performing more geological surveys. Wasting time and money if you ask me, which nobody ever does.

As it happens, my little disconnection trick is nothing less than a genius move. I am singing, my loud, out of tune voice reverberating around inside my helmet. It would be more amusing if everyone could hear me, but my voice isn't what I want to go viral on national television. Nope, not at all. My actions are what is important. Viewers will hopefully have the advantage of the carefully controlled voices of Mission Control slowly losing their shit as the auditory backdrop to my daring and adventure.

Don't get me wrong, I love the moon, the sheer pleasure of being on the surface and looking outward, of seeing Earth in all her spherical beauty. The problem, as I see it, is my belief, centred in the very core of my being, that I was made for something more. The moon isn't, by any stretch of the imagination, going to make me famous or stand out as an extraordinary human being. I would only be one more astronaut to land on it. Another of many who, for the most part, would be forgotten, if only because we were not the first.

Mars is my dream. No other journey can compete for being able to place my name in the annals of history for all to remember. No matter the outcome - tragedy or success – my fame is guaranteed because I would have been part of the first voyage. With Mars off the immediate timeline, the only way I will be remembered now is if I do something out of the ordinary, something so completely unexpected it will have millions of viewers glued to their televisions or devices across the globe.

Returning to the moon and the proposed Mars discovery mission were all part of the *Let's make NASA Great Again* campaign, a chintzy, self-serving program of propaganda and misinformation. I almost lost my cool the first time I saw the media release. It was during a round table discussion with members of congress, top brass at NASA, and the five chosen ones, me along with them.

If nothing else, I have great control and can smile and nod my way through anything. All words coming out of my mouth are those required to fit the circumstance and make it through another meeting, interview, or media interest story. I know all the right lines, gestures and facial expressions and have them down to a fine art due to the hours spent practicing in front of a mirror. Nobody, I mean nobody, ever knew what was really going on inside my sneaky little brain.

I admit, it has been harder to do of late. What, with the blatant incompetence, the red tape, NASA's play safe motto. Space isn't safe. Never has been, never will be. No amount of delay is going to prevent things from going wrong, people from dying. People die all the time, in every type of man-made transport created. Yet, I don't see cars being banned, passenger trains decommissioned, or the multitude of commercial airlines shut down.

My fundamental goal is to show them all the sheer risk of the human space venture, the formidable consequences of trusting others and believing in them. I will unequivocally demonstrate they can send people out to space, but there is never a guarantee all will return, no matter how safe they try to make it.

This launch was not supposed to go to the moon. No, no, no. The moon, along with all the human junk out there, was to by bypassed. There were to be no stops and no messing around. Gone, gone, gone. Closing my eyes allows me to visualize all the possibilities of countless days in spacetime, the final years of my life spent living out my destiny while everyone on Earth follow the odyssey, day by day.

The time spent in the dome, the endless counselling and psychiatric evaluations I had to endure. All the training, sacrifice, and preparation for nothing. So much for positive thinking, for seeing the silver cloud, posting affirmations all over my apartment and all the other stuff I talked myself into doing. One of my last acts the night before launch was a bonfire, all those hokey books and my trust along with them went up in flames.

"Well, we believe Mars is unattainable at this time. We are still looking at it... maybe in ten or twenty years."

One of the more memorable lines given by my superiors, the cowards. Spoken with all the bumbling incompetence and rhetoric management seems particularly capable of. That one line became a constant refrain in my head, a broken record of disappointment. I took to mimicking the voice and tone of each person who stood in the way of my dream, all the way up to the President of the U.S.A. An exercise that became my primary source of entertainment: morning, noon and night.

Withdrawing from public life was essential to avoid letting anything slip, possibly after one too many cocktails. All my carefully rehearsed soundbites were the only words I delivered to anyone who asked questions or tried to break my exterior of self-control.

"Busy preparing for this voyage, likely to be my last," was my retort to any enquiry about my newly acquired hermit lifestyle.

There are those who will choose to believe I am being impatient. What particularly pleases me is to imagine the panels who will discuss and dissect my decisions. Ten more years, why couldn't he wait? Well sonny, I might say, with all the condescension shown to me when I ask dumb questions, I will no longer be considered age appropriate in two years, let alone ten or, god forbid, twenty. A ruse by NASA is what it boils down to, one designed to intentionally sideline me so younger, more hopeful up and coming superstars can take my place.

I can see it now. How they would have put me in the category of mentoring astronaut. You know the ones, the old astronauts who stand at the front of the room teaching everything they know to the next generation. Spewing all their hard-earned knowledge and wisdom out to a group of entitled shits who think they know better. All before they sit back and watch some kid barely out of diapers take all the glory. Not a chance. I am a pioneer, an explorer, a traveller. It is well beyond time these little attributes of mine are recognized and applauded.

So rather than a slow decline into obscurity, I choose a flight of eternity. A deep space death launched from the moon itself. The first suicide in space has a melodic ring to it, or so I think. Once the idea came to me, I couldn't ignore it. Now, lo and behold, here I am carrying it out, proof I was able to keep up my deceit as a model member of the NASA space team until the very end.

Right after the door opened and we emerged from the capsule, I made a beeline for a buggy. Well before the rest of those morons could figure out what was going on, I'd jumped in and scooted off, leaving them choking in my moon dust. I bumped along quite happily, getting some distance between me and the landing site. Once I had a good head start, I stopped to jerry rig the vehicle, enabling it to propel itself forward at full speed without my intervention.

As I see it, all eyes of the world were on me as soon as I decamped from the others. It seems unfathomable I would not be the full point of focus, thanks to the personal cameras NASA deemed necessary to put on the top of our helmets. Moon buggy clipping along, I stood on the seat, geared up my rocket pack and used my foot to steer the vehicle towards a large crater. When it hit the lip, I launched myself into the air, giving the rocket pack full power.

Sure, there were fears, scenarios where everything went wrong danced in my head over the past months. The one most consistently playing out was being held captive by the moon's orbit, not able to get enough momentum to propel me beyond it. As usual, my fears were unjustified, so much anxiety for nothing. To be truthful, I feel only love for that moon buggy - probably still down there spinning its' wheels - and my rocket pack, which truly gave a hero's performance.

I am out here now, well out of reach of the moon's gravitational pull, my pack still propelling me forward, free and unencumbered. Whoever invented these things should be given the Nobel Prize, they are incredible. Enjoying the serenity and beauty of open space is my reward while I wait for the minutes left in my oxygen tank to count down to zero. Deep in my heart, I know I have instantly become a media sensation. It is a sweet, sweet feeling that reverberates throughout my entire body.

5 EMERGENCY EXIT

The day the chickens got loose and ran wild all over our humble settlement, located on one of the outlying moons in Sector 62, was also the day of the explosion, the one that knocked a hole the size of a football field into the ceiling of the large biodome. Old Neville Johnson, the keeper of the chickens, was nowhere to be seen while the settlement residents scrambled around trying to round up the wayward birds, which put up a fight, pecking and clawing for all they were worth. The irony was that by the end of the day the settlement had lost every single one of those chickens, each of them sucked out of the hole in the dome, a squawking cacophony of feathers and beaks. Surprisingly, only twenty residents were lost, albeit some of the best we had. Had the explosion occurred earlier in the day, the number would have been much higher. Now, without the chickens, food will be considerably less varied.

Neville, unfortunately, did not ascend into deep space death with his flightless charges. No, Neville was found curled up behind the tomato beds in the vegetable biodome. When discovered, he had a mostly empty bottle of Riley McCormick's hooch under his arm and was cuddling it like a child would a teddy bear. Our previous Commander - Riley, the maker of the best hooch in any settlement from here to Earth - was in the big dome at the time of the explosion and, subsequently, did not have to endure Amber's wrath when it came raining down.

Our current Commander, Amber Laine, was not a person many would like to cross. She was sent here, much to her displeasure, in order to clean up shop, so to speak. To be honest, we all resented Amber when she first arrived, life had been so much easier under Riley. The 167 residents of this community enjoyed his laid-back approach towards day to day life. If the atmosphere machines kept everything cozy, there was enough to eat, and the power was working, he didn't much care how we spent our days. Nope,

Riley was a live and let live kind of guy. Only now are we beginning to understand how that kind of attitude can lead to a mess such as the one occurring today. Yes sir, we are beginning to comprehend - as Amber would so succinctly put it - that we have been courting disaster because, lo and behold, it is now upon us. To put it mildly, without the large dome operational, we are in deep shit.

There are some who will argue it would have been better if Amber had been among the twenty who were lost. I don't think so. I consider it a stroke of luck she was not in the large dome. Most the residents were huddled over their late dinners - delayed on account of the chickens - our heads held low over our food, shovelling that slop into our mouths like we hadn't been fed in a month.

To say we lost our twenty best people would be an understatement, we pretty much lost all but five of the people who had been keeping this settlement going, who had been the work horses. Many still considered them traitors, these instigators who reported Riley to central headquarters. Riley wasn't one of them, he was in Amber's camp from the start and more than happy to hand over the reins of control to her, always aware of what his strengths and weakness were, along with the fact he had more of the latter than former. He was heard to say to anyone who would listen that he was never suited to the position of Commander, didn't wanted the position in the first place. It was Riley's father who wanted him to have it, wanted him to prove, once and for all, that he could grow up and be a man.

Riley wasn't having any of that, when he was deep in the clutches of his own brew, he would sit slumped in his chair and raise a weak fist in defiance. Even though his words were often slurred, his message never varied. He'd been defying his father since he was old enough to walk and, goddammit, he wasn't going to stop now. That was his motto until today, the day he died, and it never altered. Everyone knew it, the only one who never seemed to believe it was his father.

Now, so to speak, Amber had lost her support group, the ones who had her back. Within moments after the explosion, young Macauley, Deidre at his side, had a small smile playing around his lips and was whispering urgently to those on either side. While most of us were sitting in stunned silence, some of us with spoons halfway to our mouths, he was starting to put his warped plans into action. No thought as to what might have happened, if anyone had died - ruthless is Macauley - just how he could, with the boom of the explosion still ringing in our ears, play his hand and take over control of the settlement.

To be frank, I never understood the attraction of Macauley, he always seemed like a bad egg to me, but people flocked around eager to join his group, staring up at him with wide-eyed awe. Not that he wasn't handsome, sure he was. He also had a charismatic spirit that could lure in a crowd. The trick is to listen closely, when you do his words don't amount to much and, to be honest, I think he might be a little crazy.

Deidre is another wild and uncontainable spirit. With her tangled, long, blond hair and lush, puckered lips, she is a firestorm of beauty and coyness. When she first arrived, she had most of the men following her around like lost dogs, much to the chagrin of the wives. Her game - this is what I overheard Alexis say to Tamara one day - was to play people off each other, considering it nothing less than pure entertainment when it came time for them to fight it out. It was clear enough though, even to a dunce like me, it was always going to be Macauley who would win. Not that their relationship wasn't fraught, the screaming matches always played out on a central stage. Both Deidre and Macauley like an audience, for their best and worst moments.

They have come to call me Amber's puppy dog. I don't mind much; it is among the milder types of aggression thrown my way. Being called something or another and on the receiving end of endless pranks and practical jokes is my lot in life. My diminutive frame, early balding head and club foot make me an easy target. Our settlement is a collection of misfits, the bullies and bullied all crowded together under a few substandard biodomes. This is where they send you if you've had one too many blunders or aren't showing much promise.

Our small moon isn't so much a prison as the end of the road for those on the path to nowhere. The problem with that, see, is if you have too many oddballs in one area of habitation, well the entire place becomes a bit nonconformist. There are those who come into their own after being sent here, that would be the twenty we lost today, but most just amble along inside their wayward skins blaming everyone and everything rather than themselves for their misfortune. For that reason, it is an adult only settlement. The powers that be, in one of their better judgements, deemed it inappropriate to have children in such a place.

Amber though, she is fascinating. I've never seen anyone who carried so much natural power within them, who walks through life with such a high degree of confidence and self-worth. Striking to look at, with long, black hair that hangs in curls almost to her butt, she always walks at full speed, those curls bouncing along her back in a rhythmic swing that is hypnotizing. Even those with normal legs and feet have trouble keeping up with her when she is on the move.

Tall, towering over most of us, she holds herself straight without being rigid. To say that my initial awe and fear of her turned into a crush would not be far from the truth. Despite the whispers, I am content with any scraps of attention she throws my way, which are mostly in the form of work. Since Amber, with Roger at her side, does little else other than work, I rarely feel excluded.

Once over the initial shock of the explosion, I got up, leaving my food half finished, and limped out of the dining area. About a dozen others followed me, all the ones I expected to step up in times of trouble. They are the ones that don't like to rock the boat, who keep their heads down and do as they are told. The ones who have a conscience, albeit, not always visible until there is a crisis.

As I swung out the door and turned into the corridor taking me to the executive wing, I saw Macauley's cold eyes summing up those who were leaving, one of his cronies reciting names out loud, using his fingers to count them off. I figured, wrongly, he wouldn't be much trouble today and led the way to the control centre. We found Amber, Roger, Jose, Cherise and Isabel entrenched in an intense discussion. Our little ragtag group crowded into the doorway of the room, silent and watchful like sheep waiting to be herded.

Amber looked over and spied me, "oh good, Stu, you can be our record keeper."

I scuttled over to the computer and placed myself in front of it. Computers are where I do my best work, my foot hidden from view as I create binary acrobatics.

"I need three people to suit up with Jose and go investigate what went wrong." Amber regarded the group. "Stanley, if you wouldn't mind, it would be good to have a mechanic on this."

Stanley, a large middle-aged man with a potbelly, stepped forward after the smallest of hesitations. His wife, Carol, was standing beside him and her mouth formed a little oh shape without any sound coming out. It was only momentary, this little betrayal of fear and uncertainty, then she composed herself and stepped forward to stand beside her husband.

Pursing her lips, a gesture Amber makes when considering her next words carefully, she regarded the couple before very gently saying, "Carol, I'd rather have you here for now."

Amber stood up to get a better view when it became clear nobody else was going to offer their services, "Mikhail and Lindy, could you join?"

I was watching over the top of the computer, typing in names of all those present. Carol's face had altered shaped again, a creased and worried look on it while clutching Stanley's arm with a death grip. Lindy and Mikhail joined Jose without speaking. This is usually the way here, most won't volunteer for anything, only preforming the duties outlined in their position requirements and no more. Not that there aren't those who will do extra work, the rub is they must be asked directly first.

After Isabel walked over and carefully detached Carol from Stanley's arm, Jose led his group out and down the corridor to where the suits were kept. When they returned several hours later, they brought with them a small section of hose, which had a fine, deliberately cut incision in it. The group in the control centre had, by this time, dwindled down to eight people. Amber had sent the rest off to get some sleep. The only one who refused this directive was Carol, insisting she would wait until her husband returned safe and sound, thank-you very much.

All gathered around the large conference table where Jose placed the piece of hose in front of him. The discussion regarding the ramifications of this discovery was just starting when heavy, fast footsteps were heard in the hallway. A few moments later, Dylan burst through the door. He was breathing hard, and it looked like he had been dragging and carrying old Neville with him the entire way. Once Neville was released, he staggered around, bobbing and weaving in a circle while uttering little cries of complaint.

Locating a wall, Neville collapsed against it and looked up, giving Dylan the evil eye, "there was no call for all that son, dragging me all over the settlement. I thought you was taking me to my cabin."

Finally clueing into the fact there were others in the room, and he was the centre of attention, Neville looked around. When he caught sight of Amber, a little spark of fear glimmered in his eyes. He leaned forward, stage whispering to Dylan, "what in hell's name did you bring me here for?" Jerking his head toward Amber, "lady boss don't like me much, you know."

Dylan, bent over double with hands on his knees trying to calm his breathing, ignored Neville. Once under control, he looked up and addressed Amber directly.

"Trouble brewing."

"What sort."

"The Macauley sort."

Roger leaned over and picked up the piece of tubing, "not wasting time is he." He waved the tubing back and forth for effect, "bet he's behind this."

"Possibly," says Amber.

She looked back to Dylan, "weapons?"

"Keiflan is with them."

I gave a little wince. Loves weapons does Keiflan, likes to make them out of scraps. Since none of the residents are permitted firearms, he makes do with creating his own, spending his days off outside in the junk heap. Rumour has it he has quite a collection, although I've never known anyone to claim they've seen it with their own eyes. Keiflan doesn't like the company of others, prefers to be on his own. When he does talk, though, it is always about weapons, how he could use almost anything he holds as one.

What gives Keiflan extra privileges are the sculptures he creates, which have become popular as far as Sector 55. Some are dotted here and there around our own settlement, the ones Keiflan considers failures and won't sell. Otherwise, he's made himself a tidy profit selling his stuff to other settlements, which is why he has clearance to be at the dump whenever he wants.

"Not good," said Roger, "not good at all. What's in it for Keiflan?"

A shrug from Dylan, "can never tell with him, he always seems to be on a different path."

"Right there," agreed Amber. "We'll assume the rumours are true. We don't have much time I suspect."

Dylan waved his hand at that, "you have a little, they all went to get some kip, that's how I got away, saying I'd take care of Neville." He waved vaguely at the supine form of Neville, who, once determining he was off the hot seat, had rolled up into a fetal position on the floor, partially blocking the doorway, and started a low, whistling snore. "They think they will be more successful if they hit early in the morning, seem to know you lot are still up and figure you won't sleep at all tonight, giving them an advantage."

Cherise gave a little snort at this, "Macauley, what a piece of work. I told you Amber, you should have dealt with him right when you got here."

"Okay, Cherise," Amber said with a sigh, "I got it. I was wrong, thought you were bitter because he chose Deidre over you."

Cherise tossed her head, "hardly."

Carol was holding onto Stanley like he'd survived a near death experience and was trying to tug him out of the room. Easily twice the size of his wife, Stanley was holding his ground. We were all tired and stressed, and, with this news, all looking toward Amber for the next decision.

Isabel ran her hands through her hair, tugging at it, resulting in her short hair standing straight up, a common look for Isabel when she was thinking through a problem. She paced a bit and then said, "we'll have to risk taking the shuttle. The Cyclone is too small, will only take five tops and we have, what, eighteen now. I can have it ready in two hours."

"I thought there was an issue with the coolant system?" Roger queried Isabel.

"Yeah, I've been working on it since the last cancelled flight. I believe she'll be able to take off and get us out of orbit. We might have to shut down and float if we need to do repairs, but it should be okay if we get her moving in the right direction."

"Risky," replied Roger.

Isabel only shrugged, "have a better idea?"

She took the silence as a no and headed for the door. Just before walking out, she turned back, "I'll wake Ivor and have him disable the Cyclone, since we don't have enough trained pilots and navigators in this group to take both ships. Then, at least, nobody can follow us."

"Good idea. We'll organize on this end," Amber checked her

communication device, "and meet you there at 0300 hours."

That is how we ended up leaving in the dead of night, like outcasts and thieves. We gained altitude before giving those old, worn out engines as much power as they could take and limped away. I watched the settlement, a place I've lived in for the past twenty-two years but never considered home, slowly growing smaller.

Now here I am, sitting in a too large shuttle, three seats all to myself and feeling a little lost. Isabel and Ivor are in the cockpit and young Janey has joined them. The rest are all huddled up in singles or pairs, lying across seats or on the floor, wrapped in blankets, asleep or dozing. I can hear Amber and Roger near the back, it sounds like they are locked into one of their intense discussions. They spend much of their time this way, talking seriously, the conversation often meandering off into tangents, weaving away along paths I am unable to follow.

It finally occurred to me today, in the aftermath of the explosion, that they are lovers. I am still a little unsettled by it, not because I thought I had any chance, not by a long shot, but because I am unable to imagine it. They are both so efficient that it is difficult to see either playing the romantic role, certainly not the way Deidre gazes adoringly at Macauley. I am beginning to see their partnership is better, based less on physicality and more on respect for the other.

I unbuckle my seatbelt and move towards them. I sit on a small, fold-down seat across the aisle and turn to peer out the oval window beside me, staring at the black distance beyond while waiting for them to acknowledge me. There is a slight pause in the conversation between Amber and Roger, and I feel their eyes on me but, even with questions burning in my throat, it is difficult to speak.

After several moments, I hear Amber's voice, low and relaxed, "have you ever wondered about the different trajectories of your life, where you might be right now had you said yes rather than no at certain times? Or the other way around?"

I am watching them in my peripheral vision and Roger reaches over to grasps her hand, the first instance of public affection I've witnessed between them, "No way. Miss these dramatic little exits you seem to favour."

"Oh, come now, they aren't all this bad."

"What will happen down there?" My voice is low, the question mumbled into the window because I'm not certain I want to know the answer.

"Oh, death. The slow and painful kind resulting from starvation or the quick and violent kind when tensions start running high." Amber raises her hands to gather that thick, lush hair up and twist it into a messy ponytail, "their choice."

"No rescue?"

"Nope. I always wonder what these little would-be anarchic leaders are thinking." Amber is shaking her head at the thought of it.

"Like the Cyrion Asteroid?"

"Just like that," says Roger.

Twisting my body around awkwardly, I stare at them, trying to comprehend the ramifications of their words. This time it will be people I lived and worked with, not unknowns on some place I never went. My vision is going blurry and I feel nauseous from fatigue. There are flashing star shapes in my peripheral vision, a sign of a migraine to come. Amber gets up and comes over to me, placing one of her hands on my shoulder.

"It's been a long day, Stu. Try to get some rest. The fun isn't over yet."

I nod, try to think about how it will be for us and for those we left behind. There is no certainty we will make it to our destination, a planet about three days from here. Those left behind might rejoice at first, probably speeding up their end considerably by wasting what food is left in a reckless celebration that will be all about Macauley. I wonder what will happen when the first food transport doesn't show up, when none of their pleas are answered. My imagination is not up to the task and I bid Amber and Roger goodnight and stumble down to the open area, find a spare corner on the floor, grab a blanket and fall into a fitful sleep, my dreams disturbed by disasters large and small.

6 PLAYING PREY

Tottering on my three-inch stilettos, I create a display of incompetence at the roadside turnout, a couple of long-haul drivers and a pickup with three hunters taking amused notice. Timmins, a long-haired chihuahua with a pink crystal rhinestone collar, follows beside my ankle dragging her leash. Popping the hood, I lean over, feeling my skin-tight, white skirt move up a few inches. Shrugging, I push the hood with the base of my palm to close it, careful not to scratch my newly polished nails.

Kneeling, I gather Timmins in my arms and coo to her as I pull open the driver's side door, which sticks when halfway open. Giving my hip a dramatic swing, I shove it until it gives the telltale crunch of something long past it's sell-by date and cranks to fully open. Climbing into my battered, rusted 1999 Honda Civic, I rev it up, watching the blue smoke emit from the tailpipe, and putter off into the slow lane, not bothering to signal.

Fifty feet down the road I flick on my hazards and turn onto a barely visible dirt road, climb a small rise and disappear from sight of the highway. Long, dry grass hems in the track on both sides and down the middle of the two ruts. A neutral zone exists between two sections of private land, flanked on either side by barbed wire fences, the place a fire in the making.

Leaving the car, Timmins and I walk down the track, my heels sinking into the soft dirt. I sense rather than hear the Dodge Ram 3500 pickup leave the pullout I recently left. Blissfully, without a care in the world, Timmins and I carry on, walking slowly, oozing vulnerability. The men take their time, their dually, four-wheel drive truck easily navigating the barely perceptible roadway. We are a quarter mile along the path when I hear the truck rumble over the rise and stop, blocking in my vehicle. Sounds of distant traffic, prairie, and the echoing silence inside my head are invaded by three doors slamming shut. With the wind behind me, their cheerful tones of disbelief at my stupidity easily carry to my ears.

The question is, who is the target? It is true, I'd seen them earlier in the day at a service station, fueling up and catcalling to every woman in sight, ridiculing the men, cruising for trouble. Gun rack visible along the back window, they swaggered in their newly bought camo outfits and loudly vocalized their murderous intentions to any living animal foolish enough to cross their path.

They saw me, but not the way I present myself now. My vehicle was an SUV, Timmins a springer spaniel following on my heels. In rugged boots, jeans and a down vest, I appeared as someone out hiking for the day. In terms of attractiveness, there was none to speak of. Hair pulled back from my face, nose too wide, eyes unadorned and unremarkable, body squat and square. Even so, they whistled as I walked by and Timmins turned her head to bare her teeth at them. A warning they chose to laugh at rather than take seriously.

With a guffaw, the largest one leaned over slightly, "ooh, there's a vicious one. Come on over here little lady so we can give your dog something to snarl at."

Muscles easily visible through the clothing he wore, arrogance cloaked over him with reckless ferocity, he was a man not easily intimidated, one who considered the world his oyster and he there to steal it. Shaggy beard beside him gave out a loud roar of hilarity, so revved up on testosterone, anything was funny. The third, his bald head shining in the noonday sun, cigarette hanging from the corner of his mouth, cocked his eyebrow, leering with unkind intentions.

I kept walking across the already hot asphalt, taking their measure, deciding they were nothing less than perfect. Climbing back in my SUV, the men's attention was diverted by the arrival of new vehicles. When they left, we followed, the SUV transforming into the Honda on a blind corner, out of sight and mind.

Taking a moment to feel the late summer breeze on my face and absorb the rustle of grain close to harvesting, I close my eyes and smile. Glancing over, I catch Timmins eye and she winks in her lackadaisical, doggy way. Together, we turn around to face our foe, breaking into a run at the same time, our gaits perfectly matched.

For my part, there is little change. Shoes kicked off, my bare feet easily avoid golfer and badger holes alike. Skirt lengthening, it and opens wide to become a cape of flowing white behind me. Timmins, on the other hand, is beauty in motion. Within five steps she has outgrown her chihuahua guise and is closer to a shih tzu, her mouth spread back showing spiked canines and a growl rocking the ground like thunder, a tiny lion let loose.

At the truck, the men haven't noticed. They are huddled together making plans, outlining their attack, drawing straws on who gets first dibs. Shaggy beard glances over his shoulders and nudges the others with his elbows. Lazily, big grins on their wide, stupid faces, they turn to watch us approach. The largest crosses his arms over his chest and takes a wider stance, a human barricade of manliness. Baldy holds his arms out in front, fingers wiggling us onward. Come to us, baby, they are saying.

Over the next few strides, I feel my legs lengthen and Timmins shapes herself into a border collie, running circles around me so as not to arrive first. She throws up dust devils that race off in an outward direction, creating an ever-widening circle of chaotic energy. Halfway there, the men's faces start to show confusion. There is no stopping this train, we are full speed ahead and coming in fast.

Shaggy beard takes a step or two backward, stumbling on the exposed root of a sagebrush. He sprawls backwards on his behind and his companions can't help but smirk at him. It is what their friendship is based on, belittling each other and the world around them. Within their moment of distraction, Timmins moves into wolfhound mode and my hair lets loose, flying behind me, the ends reaching out to taste the air and gather momentum.

Timmins circles wide, aiming for the hood of the truck, her appearance navigating into mythical while her mouth pulls back into a sneer, saliva dripping in a long strand from the corners, eyes blazing red and gold. Her paws are dinnerplates, causing four- inch dents in the grey hood of the truck. Without pausing, she bounds on the roof, which buckles slightly.

There is no long moment of suspense where she leans over the edge of the truck and takes the measure of her quarry, watching them quiver in their boots and piss themselves. Not Timmins, no slow-motion movie spectacle here, she makes a smooth glide downward, her head becoming the size of a tractor wheel with the movement, her mouth spread wide to swallow whole shaggy beard and baldy.

Muscle man is mine alone. His arms are still crossed casually over his chest, his eyes glint a threat. When I'm five paces away, still picking up speed, he opens his arms wide as though to catch me in an embrace. I slice right through him, letting him see at the last instant the hollowness of my eyes, the flash of one semblance of eternity. The penetration of his body causes it to evaporate, the molecules gathering into a long rope and rising skyward. Apex reached, they arc back down, a blue glow of pure energy.

Standing straight, I wait for an influx of feeding, which hits my spine with a rush and infuses me with new vitality. The sensation is something between shock and orgasm and I shudder upon impact. My throat betrays pleasure with an audible moan, while my head is thrown back, eyes closed in surrender. No time to linger, the job must be finished, the dust devils are returning for their reward.

Opening my eyes, I see Timmins is once more a long-haired chihuahua, daintily cleaning her front, right paw, rhinestone collar and leash back in place. Kneeling into a squat, I call her to me, and she trots over to accept a scratch behind the ears. Leash in hand, I glide back to standing and we return to our vehicle, now a jeep with no roof and extra wide tires.

The last remaining evidence of our encounter must be removed. Revving the jeep to life, I twist my body around and aim a rocket straight at the midafternoon sun glinting off the windows of the pickup. Into action on impact, the rocket first heats the truck toward molten red before plunging it into sub-zero temperatures. Jumping into the back seat, tail wagging with expectation, Timmins spits a dart from her mouth at the hood of the truck as I hit the accelerator and we gun it down the laneway. The frozen Dodge shatters into infinitesimal fragments, the dust devils moving in to suck everything up, clearing the space of all evidence.

Pulling sharply on the parking brake, we perform a neat 180-degree turn, and blaze back toward the highway. Slowing to a crawl, we creep over the rise, now driving a silver two-seater convertible Mercedes. Indicator on and clicking rhythmically, we approach the battered stop sign. I stroke the top of Timmins silky head, my acknowledgement of a job well done while waiting for a break in traffic.

There are no backward glances, life is an ever-advancing march onward. Highway momentarily empty, I give the vehicle free reign as we regain asphalt. Pulling back after a minute, I slow the car down. Not wishing to attract unwanted law enforcement attention, we cruise at the speed limit, fingers thrumming on the steering wheel, Timmins head bouncing with the rhythm of some rock song belting out from the stereo.

I allow myself a triumphant smile, it really was too easy. Men, you know, should really be more careful on these deserted laneways.

7 BROKEN CIRCLES

An ordinary life is what I've lived. Not overly fantastic or glamorous but not a complete disappointment. There have been exciting moments, successes, failures, ups and downs. My name was briefly known for a short period about twenty years ago, after the release of my first and last book. Now I write in solitary obscurity, not wishing anyone to read the words I place on paper, refusing to ever again face the hassle of the public eye.

With incredulous amusement, I have read books about my book. These so-called scholars have torn it apart, paragraph by paragraph, their interpretations so far off the mark I laugh out loud. Makes me glad I never wasted my time and money on a post-secondary education, if the primary result is spewing out such horseshit. Let me set the record straight once and for all, it was a simple story made up in my head, mostly out of a growing dissatisfaction with my life.

Blessed with an active imagination, I allowed it to run riot. That's it. I was not intentionally challenging any paradigms. I didn't know then, and still do not, fully comprehend the definition of an archetype, so I certainly wasn't invoking any into my novel. My book was a jaded, middle-aged woman's escape from the realities of her day to day existence. Nothing more. Do yourselves a favour and move on to examining a piece of literature worth the effort.

At 79 years old, I believe I've earned the right to voice my opinion. Those who don't like it can lump it. It's so very dreary playing nice all the time. People, let me tell you, do not like honesty. I love it myself, makes me want to stand and yell halleluiah when I meet another who isn't afraid of voicing their true thoughts. Being mean or unkind is not necessary, but don't lie just because it seems the polite thing to do.

Long time ago, in my misspent youth, I worked in a fire camp where we each took turns cooking. There was one girl there who couldn't cook to save her soul. She openly admitted this, but group thinking demanded she take her turn. There are many things to attempt when starting out your cooking life, a simple macaroni and cheese or maybe a casserole of some sort. Quiche, on the other hand, isn't one of them. In my memory, long aged, it remains one of the worst things I ever tasted. The pastry like cardboard, no seasoning used, the whole thing overdone.

Pushing my plate away after a single bite earned me dirty looks and words of admonishment. Everyone else ate their piece, praising this girl no end on how wonderful it was. A piece of dishonesty doing none of us any good because we had to endure her cooking once a week for the rest of the summer. Having received such praise for her quiche, it became part of her regular repertoire, and everything else she made was equally horrendous. I took to taking extra shifts in the tower, preferring bags of dried fruit and nuts to anything she would create.

Speaking of cooking, I made a lovely poppyseed cake two days ago. It will make a nice snack when I grow weary of my memories. I am writing these words as snow continues to fall outside. It is now at the bottom of the windows and still coming down. The storm rolled in a couple days ago and shows no signs of abating. Holed up in my little cabin in Nova Scotia, the snow is providing extra layers of insulation in a structure not meant to be lived in year-round.

Two weeks ago, following my last doctor's appointment, I skipped out and came here. Just packed a single bag, took a cab to the airport, bought a ticket and was airborne in no time. One thing, among many, I failed to do before leaving was to inform anyone of my intentions. Soon my children will begin to wonder where I am. Likely each of them will succumb to a state of frustrated panic because I, once again, refuse to act my age.

It gives me great pleasure to give them a taste of their own medicine. They certainly never call me when they are going away. For my own safety, don't you know, I am expected to tell them each time I step a toe outside my front door. There is a schedule, somewhere. I think I was supposed to put it on my fridge. Anyway, it clearly laid out what week belongs to which child, who is off mother duty and who is on. Maybe I recycled it.

Not the most attentive, my children. Preferably, I am to keep them posted not by a phone call, or a face to face meeting but with one of those text things. They don't have time to chat or check in on me and have a visit. The schedule and what have you is only so they can say they did their best, to shake their heads and sigh dramatically about how difficult I am.

Given, they picked up the pace when my book made the best seller list. It was all wheedling and whining though, only looking for a cut of the money. Since they felt so much of the book was based on their childhood, their claim was I owed it to them. I wasn't buying it; my experience of their childhood had nothing to do with the book I wrote.

Unlike my children, who live in houses filled to overflowing with material glut, I have become positively spartan in my lifestyle with each passing year. Right now, I am sitting on a hard, wood chair at a rickety table, both which I bought at a garage sale. The cottage is tiny, without running water, two rooms only along with a miniscule kitchen. The outhouse has been inaccessible since yesterday and I have a gardening bucket in the porch, my waste products freezing in the bottom, giving a crackle and hiss when a new delivery arrives.

The whiskey, on the other hand, is of high quality. There seems little point in drinking garbage. Smoking is a habit I took up a few years ago. Why not? Death was coming and I decided I wanted to leave this earthy plane with a few vices under my belt. Taking up these unladylike habits resulted in shock waves rolling through my small group of acquaintances, not to mention my children. The sheer outrage elicited was some of the highest quality entertainment I've had in years.

My grandchildren have followed in the footsteps of their parents. This is the price society pays for trying to be a modern parent, for pandering to their offspring rather than laying down boundaries with thick borders and no ambiguity. I do not expect daily, weekly or even monthly visits or phone calls. However, a thank-you card for a gift I have given is appreciated.

In all the years I've been a grandmother, I have never received a single one, not from any of my seven grandchildren. I suppose the blame could rest with me, for forcing my children to write those cards after every birthday and Christmas to the point where they came to loathe them. Their children are growing up and starting to leave home, they will find out soon enough what it feels like.

Outside my immediate family, there are numerous cousins who have been circling like vultures for years waiting for me to kick the bucket, hoping for a windfall from the reading of my will. Hate to disappoint, but they'll get none of it. All my money will pass to a literary foundation. Rather than benefit a handful of selfish, ungrateful people who lay claim simply because we are related by blood, I choose to benefit those I don't know. It is amusing to watch my extended family pander and grovel. They must think I forget the years of neglect, the disdain and impatience displayed towards me at every family function for being different and forging along paths not well tread.

I've been called a miser in my time. Each of us is called so many things over the course of our lives and some are stickier than others. Eleven years old and I received more money than gifts for my birthday. Don't know why, perhaps I was being difficult, and nobody knew what to do with me. In my mind's eye I can see my exasperated mother wearily telling relatives and friends to give money and let me figure out what I want. I don't know if this happened, but I can imagine something to that effect being so. My mother never understood me; I was always too far outside normal for her.

My eldest sister decided, in her own brand of 13-year-old wisdom, I should spend all my money on things she wanted. When I refused, she hurled abuse at me. Miser was the one she badgered me with most consistently. Hissed at me first thing in the morning, the back of my head smacked with the flat of her hand for good measure. To hammer the point home, I was followed when walking to school, the taunting continued by her and a collection of the popular crowd she hung out with.

After a week, I finally gave in and handed the money over to her. It earned me triumph laced with disdain, marked forever as an easy target. The gift my money bought was candy for her gang of friends, none of it shared with me or our other siblings. When she died of a drug overdose in her early twenties, I couldn't drum up a single tear for her.

People can think what they want, but I give money away all the time to charities and homeless people. There was an old guy I used to see regularly downtown. A white beard, unkempt and scraggly, hung halfway down his chest and ended in a tattered point. Hair, the same colour and condition, was always covered by some sort of hat or cap.

Standing on one corner or another, always a different one, he would stamp his foot and call out the same sentence over and over in a toneless chant. His voice had ragged edges to it and, while the words were incoherent, the message was clear. Help, I am homeless and hungry. Each time I saw him, I gave whatever money I had, always reminding myself to carry more cash but the thought slipping from my brain minutes later.

On a particularly cold winter day, the kind where it was painful to be outside for more than ten minutes, I almost didn't see him as I passed. It was his familiar monotone that caused me to look up from the ground, peer around the trim of my hood. The old man had on runners open at the toes, the bottom flapping when he moved his foot up and down in rhythm to his call. Completing the ensemble was a ripped coat and too short jeans.

Opening my wallet, I gave him all the money I had, which probably wasn't more than thirty dollars – who carried cash even back then - and skipped lunch so I could buy him better clothes. When I came back with the bag fifteen minutes later, he was gone, and I never saw him again. These are the things my heart breaks over, the ones I feel so hopeless in the face of, believing as though nothing I did was ever enough.

Living this long, it is my choice to determine when and how I die. The natural death is over-rated. My last years will not be ones where I am cared for, ever more incompetent and incapable, by people I don't know. While I am still of sound mind – a point my children might disagree on – I wish to make this decision myself. The exact moment of death is unknown but is approaching soon. I can almost taste it.

All the whiskey is gone, and the snow is now halfway up the window.

My feet are numb from sitting too long at this table, I believe it's time for a break. Upon my arrival, I pulled the table into my small living area to be close to the wood burning stove, my sole source of warmth. The couch is on the other side of the stove, where I have been sleeping for short stretches, those eight to ten-hour nights of sleep from my youth are now only a distant memory.

Even without my irresponsible bladder, the chill has been waking me, informing me it is time to get up and place more wood on the fire. My creaky, old bones protest, but I do it anyway. Enough now, no more of this day to day stuff. This journal is about working through my memories, not boring myself with trivial nonsense. My pen must stop. Time to brave the cold of the kitchen for a cup of tea and a piece of my beautiful poppyseed loaf.

The old woman lifts a coat off a hook and puts it on, having trouble with the buttons, which she can no longer see and must manage blindly with shaking hands. A second pair of thick, down booties are placed over the thin ones she already wears. Using the wall for support, she pushes on the kitchen door with her hip, which sticks slightly along one edge.

Over the past few years, her sense of smell has steadily declined and today she is unable to detect the gas as she enters the kitchen. The stove is ancient, and the pilot light often blows out when the burner is off. A point she is aware of, but in her hurry to return to the much warmer room on the other side of the door, she doesn't bother to check.

Unwrapping the poppyseed loaf made the day the storm hit, she cuts off a small piece and takes a bite, chewing slowly with eyes closed. Poppyseed loaf requires tea to accompany it. A half a jug of water sits on the counter and she carefully lifts it with both hands, thinking to herself she will have to open a window and start collecting snow tomorrow.

The water in the kettle has ice crystals floating on top, so she swirls it around before topping it off with water from the jug. Her arm stretches for the box of matches sitting on a small shelf over the stove, shaking them and remembering she is down to the last one and will have to dig a new box out of the overfilled pantry next time. The last thing the old woman does in this life is light that single match.

8 VISTING THE PAST

There are those who covet fame, even notoriety, I was not one of them. I never wished for my name and photo to be pasted all over the front pages of newspapers and magazines. Yet, they had been there for months, which is what called him to me. After avoiding him for more than eighteen years, I knew he would show up on my doorstep soon. My name underwent numerous changes over the past years and was not of concern. Photos of me were the issue. I had not altered my appearance dramatically and, as the years past with no sign of him, I'd gone back to my lazy look, the one he knew well. With mousy brown hair tied up in a messy ponytail, no makeup, baggy t-shirts or sweatshirts - depending on the time of year – and casual pants to cover my too long legs.

Not that he is dangerous, not in the physical sense. No, that is not the issue. He is simply threatening to my overall well-being, to my ability to have any level of contentment. Now, due to circumstances beyond my control, my life is so far off-kilter I feel crooked when I move. Driving is beyond my abilities as I am unable to hold the vehicle between the lines. I remain close to home, my employer being generous in his immediate dismissal of me. Groceries, filling prescriptions, and checking my post office box are all within easy walking distance from my house. Thinking back to the ultra- busy lifestyle I courted before my forced exile from society, I wonder what drove me.

Walking is not easy, and it is a relief I never have far to go. Unable to hold a straight course, my steps are slow and clumsy, causing my body to meander all over the sidewalk. The dog, with her lock jaw and fierce growl, is useful for keeping gawkers at a distance. Even so, hecklers always arrive, remaining on the opposite side of the street, a safe distance from which to call their disparaging remarks. It is a useless exercise for these cowards, I have learned to wear noise cancelling headphones on my outings. A new habit of mine is to not take the headphones off, as is correct, during any transactions I make, only nodding and smiling, before I pay, take my purchases and leave.

I admit, I'd been expecting him since the first day I was standing in line at the grocery store and my face stared back at me from the line of magazines next to the checkout counter. There is nothing stunning or spectacular about my appearance. A generic face with hazel eyes, button nose, high cheekbones, slightly arched eyebrows, and finely shaped mouth. Numerous times over the course of my life, a person would insist they knew someone who could be my sister. Sometimes, they would pull out photos but, I never saw any resemblance, although they always maintained it was there. Nobody would dare pollute themselves anymore by confusing me for one whom they are acquainted with, my features having gained some distinctiveness thanks to the overzealous media.

Today, I stay at the house. I braved an outing yesterday and my body remains drained from the effort. The berries are ready for harvesting, so I grab a stack of large bowls and pull open the back door. The dog rushes ahead of me, bounding into the already warm air with head held high and tail wagging. A subordinate in this decision, I hold the screen door for her, allowing it to slam shut behind us. Harvesting on my large lot is an hours long endeavor. I pick the fruit and my dog chases flies and wasps, adding a little wild protein to her diet.

By the time I couldn't pick another berry if I wanted to, I have several containers filled to overflowing and my dog is laid out under the large apple tree panting in the heat. My shoulders feel the curse of inadequate sunscreen and my head is beginning to throb due to lack of hydration. As I rise to my feet, my joints and bones protest from too long spent kneeling, I gently remind myself the remaining harvest can wait for another day or, more practically, given back to nature from whence it came.

The berries still need to be sorted and cleaned, so I take my haul out to the front deck. It is now in shade with a light breeze blowing across from the south, a welcome relief. Gently placing the filled containers near my chair, I cover them with a tea towel. Back inside, I find the dog looking from me to the front door to her bed. She opts for her bed, which is close to the ceiling fan, as I go to the kitchen for more bowls, filling one with water. As I walk back toward the front door, the dog lifts her head slightly then lets it drop, without even a whimper of interest.

Forty minutes of easy contentment follows, and I know when it abruptly ends that I should have counted the minutes more closely, enjoyed each second as though it were my last. A small rental car pulls up outside my house and I recognize him as he steps out of the vehicle. He raises his hand, a gesture I fail to return. Within me there is nothing, no joyful anticipation at the sight of him, no butterflies arousing excitement in my stomach. My emotions are a flatline of feeling and I am glad for it. It is time to end the waiting, it is time, once and for all, to get this over with.

He advances with a heavy step, a pronounced limp on his left side speaking to an injury sustained since I last saw him all those years ago. Sunglasses are casually removed as he passes into the shade while climbing the steps to my deck. Unable to prevent myself, I glance up briefly and my first impression is the years have not been kind to him. At fifty-five, he has prematurely aged with a deeply lined face and snow-white hair. Once ice blue eyes are now dull with the beginnings of cataracts, his back permanently hunched, causing him to appear shorter than he is. Not that he'd ever been particularly handsome, he was by no means a man to ogle over. His attraction was in a force of personality that drew people in, one that could infect others and leave them begging for more.

At the top of the steps he pauses, and I can feel him watching me. I do not acknowledge him nor stop my work. Eventually, in a quiet and careful voice, he says, "Leila."

"Robert."

"May I sit?"

A slight nod is encouragement enough. With no other chair nearby and me unwilling to play the gracious host, he must scout out his own seating arrangements. With a quiet sigh, he walks to the far end of the porch to collect one from around the large outdoor table sitting there. Hesitating, he eventually decides to place the chair on the opposite end of the small foldout table I am using for the berries and sits down heavily.

"Need any help?"

"That won't be necessary."

He leans back in the chair, tipping it onto the back legs, and looks from side to side. From inside I can hear the low belly rumbling of the dog, who has left the comfort of her bed to sit inside the screen door.

"Nice house you have."

Without thinking, I snort in derision and the low rumble of the dog turns to a growl. "This house is an albatross, also for sale."

Locking his raptor gaze on me with a sharp turn of the head, "surely, you will not be allowed to sell it?"

Ignoring his intensity, shrugging it off as something beneath my notice, I say, "one day."

He continues to stare at me while I refuse to look up, "I came a long way to see you, Leila, please have the courtesy to look at me."

There it was, him moving in, playing boss. "You forget, I did not invite you here."

"Nonetheless, it is not a short flight from Africa."

A short, harsh bark emits from my throat at this obvious ruse to brag, to bring to my attention how he fulfilled his dreams, to challenge me into reacting, "why did you bother returning?"

"It was time and you clearly require my assistance."

"Too late, by multiple lifetimes."

"That was not my fault."

"Naturally, tell me whose fault then?"

"Maybe it was nobody's, Leila, maybe it was the way it needed to be."

"Convenient that, I will disagree."

Attempting to quell his anger, he shakes his head from side to side, opens his knees wide and stares at the surface of the deck between them. Each of us knows the other so well and, even now, how to push each other's buttons. We sit without verbal communication for close to a quarter of an hour. This, I know, is his attempt to draw me out, one he used numerous times in the past and I would always fall for. Not anymore, solitude has taught me the art of silence, of holding my tongue and not blurting out whatever thoughts pass through my head.

Throughout this lull in our conversation, the dog continues to growl, and Robert finally speaks, "something wrong with your dog?"

"I think she doesn't like my visitor."

Not an avenue he wishes to pursue so he finally comes to the point, "I still love you."

"Controlling someone is not loving them."

"Not once did I do anything you didn't agree to."

I almost throw my bowl of berries at him. They are a deep red colour, their juice staining my hands and arms. Remembering my anger management exercises, I take a deep breath to regain my centre before I speak again. "You would have kept me out there, locked safely out of sight, for years until you were ready. Confinement was your dream for me, a locked room and nothing more."

"It wasn't quite like that."

"Are you going to deny it was not your wish?" My voice is shaking, almost a whisper to stop myself from shouting.

The neighbours have been coming out one by one. They are attempting to look nonchalant, walking by my house, throwing surreptitious glances our way, trying to get a good look at this latest stranger on my porch. Deciding, belatedly, the charade has gone on long enough, I yank my phone toward me and fire off a text message, something I should have done as soon as he arrived. Before returning my attention to the bowl of berries, I supply my neighbours with a cheery wave, throwing in a big smile for good measure.

Directly across the street from mine is a large ramshackle house and the owner – with her laugh somewhere between a donkey and a hyena – is holding court. From my porch, I can hear the growing crowd being regaled with one of her unending monologues. That woman's nasal, whining voice has been the backdrop to my six summers in this house, a person with nothing to say and a voice that never quits.

"You are somewhat popular," Robert says as his attention alters between me and the gathering across the street.

"It was bound to happen sooner or later."

He shifts, takes a new angle, "you still owe me money."

Finally, my phone dings and I delay responding to Robert until I have replied to the incoming text. "Write down your address, I will send it to you."

"You said that before."

"I wasn't ready then, I am now. You will get the cheque."

"Direct deposit is easier."

"Not for me, if you require the money then it will be by cheque." I push a pen and pad of paper towards him, one I constantly have beside me so I can write things down as I remember them.

Irritable, he says, "you can send it care of my sister, this is her address."

"You needn't worry, I will certainly not come to find you."

Throughout his visit, the cats have been randomly appearing, each of them jumping on my lap to be caressed while glaring at him with malicious intent. With a hiss directed in Robert's direction and hackles raised, they pounce down after a few minutes and run off in search of smaller prey.

"How many animals do you own?"

"None of your business, just like any other detail about my life." Now I've had a text, I can't leave my phone alone and check it again. Twenty-five minutes has elapsed since Robert arrived and yet if feels like days. Pushing him to leave is the wrong approach. His response will be to dig in and remain beyond my endurance, then move in and break me.

"I was good to you."

"Oh, is that what you call it? Is that how you are good to people? Were you being good to your wife? Are you still? Where, might I ask, is your wife?"

Here was a strategy he hated, firing off multiple questions without giving him a chance to collect his thoughts and respond. My husband disliked the practice as well; nonetheless, the habit remained. Taking his time, Robert chooses only to answer the easiest of the questions I have presented.

"I left her to go to Africa, she wouldn't come."

There it was again, Africa. He would keep dropping it into the conversation and I would continue to ignore it, "you always were a coward."

"You don't understand," he is shaking his head again.

Not once, in all the time we spent together, did he ever explain exactly what I didn't comprehend. No, his game was to pull the statement out of his hat to end a conversation, to underline the fact that he was better than me: older, wiser, the one in command.

After several minutes, I in a cool voice, "I think I understand perfectly well, I have understood for years, more than you ever gave me credit for. You live in fear, going out and chasing around these large, wild animals, pretending bravery when all you've ever done is run away from anything real."

"I'm here right now."

"Yes, except this isn't real, is it? This, right here, is you pretending, once again, to be the hero. Soon, no matter the outcome, no matter what I say or do, you will scuttle back and hide in your research."

"I know you, Leila, this bitterness does not become you."

"Oh please. You don't know me at all. That girl, that girl you think you knew, is dead. She was slain with a thousand, tiny needlepoint pinpricks until, for good measure, you ultimately stabbed her in the back."

"I'm not the one on trial here. You have warped every memory, skewed all my words. I am surprised by you."

Out of the corner of my eye I glare at him. Not achieving any satisfaction by the exercise, I pull my head back, stretching the front of my neck while my left-hand fingers massage the muscles on either side of my throat, willing my sixth chakra to remain open, to find the necessary words. Memory is a tricky thing, slippery and consumed by ego. He and I are shared memories slamming into one another, twining around in a suffocating pattern.

Dropping my head back down, I finally counter with, "they are my memories. Ones I have to do whatever I wish with."

Catching myself taking shallow and rapid breaths, I knead my left shoulder where a sharp ache has developed and mentally repeat my calming mantra, attempting to slow my heartrate and breathing, to not betray my inner turmoil by outward displays of emotion. Sitting perfectly still, his knees together and hands folded gently on his lap, a rather prim posture he prefers to adopt when he thinks he is winning the game, Robert waits me out.

Giving in, I deliver a challenge, "you are the one who came waltzing uninvited up to my house and started bringing up things better left alone. What do you want?"

"I still love you."

"The master words of manipulation. Let me remind you I was only twenty-two years old and you were, and remain, fifteen years older. There is no love in that."

"Not fair, once again. I was confused and didn't know what to do."

"Is that it? Well, I was young. You pushed and pulled me apart like I was taffy, leaving me so thin it took me years to gather myself back up again and walk forward into the world."

"How?"

"Really? The constant criticism of every single thing I did because you saw potential in me and wanted to make me better. Each time another person – colleague, employer, friend, whoever – said I had potential afterwards, I would walk away, move on, find someplace new and start over again."

"Exaggeration."

"Really? I tell you something about my life you have no way of knowing anything about and you tell me I am lying. You are the one who lied. The emails, the phone calls, the cryptic notes. You kept it up for months, even after I was gone, never letting me go. And the money, what about the money? Such an insignificant sum given the hours I worked, Yet, you bring it up. I love you, Leila. Where is my money?"

Ignoring his look of dripping empathy, I pat my knee to summon the latest cat there, give him a brief scratch behind the ears and shoo him off again. This cat is young, just over a year old, and has started testing out his dominance skills with fervour, pulling the adult cat out of his kitten fur. With a sideways walk and arched back, he hisses with frenzy at Robert. Amused by his antics, I smile, my hand reaching out unconsciously for my phone, dragging it across the discoloured table to check the time again. Three quarters of an hour now and counting. Almost done.

Robert remains silent while memories come unbidden and, more clearly than the present scene in front of me, I remember him back all those years ago standing on the side of a decommissioned road, the truck tilted so severely it was a miracle it hadn't rolled. True, it was near the end of my employment, my disillusionment with him and his research had settled into the marrow of my bored. Discordant times are easier to recall than the months before when it was mostly smooth sailing, when it was all about the project with minimal personal involvement.

The day I am recalling was another roller coaster ride. His silent treatment of the past week was over as suddenly as it had begun, and he was my best friend again. Still angry, I was acting out in my young, childish manner and had purposely taken the truck too wide around the washout, resulting in the fix we were in.

Exaggerating his masculinity, he was attempting to pull me back under his power, "I am a warrior, Leila, watch and learn."

Crouched low, his body was somewhere between ape and professional wrestler with arms flexed to show well developed biceps. Standing to full height, he growled out, "Samurai."

I smiled before dissolving into laughter, won over again. This clarification of his maleness, this proclamation given to the trees and me, brought us back into an uneasy truce. Already job hunting, my leaving was a point of constant tension. He did not choose for me to go and could not cope with me staying. My decision was firm though, he had a wife and his proclaimed love for me, which he declared in a moment of weakness days before, was driving me onward.

In hindsight, I should not have tarried, should have left in the night without notice or warning. Again, I was young, and he was a predator, his jaws holding me around the ankle and not letting me go. Nonetheless, leave I would, severing the limb and bleeding out for the next ten years.

With effort, I shake myself out of my reminiscences and return to the present. My hand sits idly in the bowl crushing a handful of berries. As is usually the case, there is too much fruit. Tomorrow, I will make preserves, much more than I need. This year, unlike in others, there will be very few willing to accept the extras as my token of friendship.

The silence continues, and I am enjoying it. I yearn for him to leave without added encouragement; however, with him, hope is always futile and his voice breaks into me, "you and I together has always been my wish. Your anger is destroying that dream. Let it go, Leila."

"What about the baby?"

Confused, he tilts his head to one side, "I suspect it is imperative to tread carefully here."

My only response is a small smile, one barely registering on my lips and not reaching my eyes.

After a few minutes, "there was no baby." Another pause, "right?"

Genuinely amused, I laugh, "oh, come now, you know as well as I we never consummated our declarations of love."

Evident relief is visible on his face, mixed with a growing frustration, "so what baby?"

"The one your wife craved with all her being."

"Okay, and…"

"How long were you married? It was her single longing, one you steadfastly denied her."

"So?"

"Rain pouring down, you and I sitting in the truck on the side of the road waiting it out. Do you remember what you said to me?"

"Yep."

"What was it?"

"You and I should have a child. I still believe that."

"As I believe your hypocrisy rules you."

"You are strong enough to forgive."

Thankfully, this is when my salvation arrives in the form of a police cruiser, which pulls up in front of my house, parking neatly behind Robert's small rental.

"Looks like you have company," he says.

Nodding, my attention fixed on the new arrival, "that would be my ongoing appointment with the law."

A tall, lean officer slowly curls his way out of the car and stands on the street for a moment, glancing over the cruiser towards my porch. He closes the driver's door and walks around the back of the vehicle to step onto the sidewalk. Resting against the closed passenger door, he crosses his feet at the ankles with arms over chest while contemplating the large trees in my front yard.

Robert leans forward, hands on knees for a few moments. He eventually stands and takes two steps to the top of the wide stairs. Pausing, he watches the street, occasionally throwing sidelong glances towards the police officer. The gathering across the road has become quiet, a hushed tension pervades the air.

Back still towards me, Robert says, "did you kill your husband Leila?"

Inhaling and exhaling to the count of ten, I remember my boundaries before responding. "Is that why you came? To ask that one asinine question? We're done here."

"It is a simple question, Leila. You invariably have difficulty answering them."

"The problem is you ask the wrong questions."

"I require honesty."

"What a fool thing to say."

"Simply answer the question."

A deep sigh before I point toward the street and the cop, "the single most important thing for me is that man, the one in the uniform standing on the street, believes me."

"An unsatisfactory answer. A mirror of my entire visit."

"It was you who determined the course of this visit years ago."

"I have never been, nor am I now, the enemy."

With that, he walks down the steps toward his rental car. I let him have the last word. He stops to talk with the officer for a time, their lips rarely moving, the stilted conversation punctuated by long silences. With a nod on both sides, Robert climbs into his rental and drives away without a backward glance or final wave. After the car disappears around the corner, the officer pushes himself up to standing and leisurely walks toward me.

9 TOXIC POISONING

When my past comes through the door of the dingy mom and pop café I work at, I am standing at a table of five with my coffee pot idle. In the booth is a family where the mother, looking haggard, has dark circles enclosing her eyes and a jaw clenched tight. Staring out at the parking lot, where the morning sun glints off cars, is the father, who clearly prefers to ignore rather than engage. Upon entering the booth, the eldest child emptied the container of sugar packets onto the table before dividing them up, taking two for each one his siblings received. Ignoring the plaintive squeaks of their mother, one sugar packet after another is opened and grubby fingers reach inside to emerge glistening white, the sweetness sucked off like sherbet.

Between licking sugar off his fingers, the older boy is keeping up a running commentary about the cut on his hand and the inadequacy of the bandage applied earlier, "I'm feeling a little faint." He looks at his mother with wide-eyed innocence, a mischievous nature shining through the ruse, "I might bleed out and you don't even care."

"Oh shut-up, Cam," the father says without adverting his eyes from the window, "or I'll give you something to feel faint about."

Waving off the apologies of the mother for making me wait, I wish every nuance of the scene back into my life. The petty complaints of three children, a husband off in his own world who joins in only to lay down his law. It is the sheer exhaustion of being a mother I miss. Once a mother always a mother, but the day all my children, along with my husband, were laid to rest side by side veered the course of my life off in a different direction. The ensuing years have been ones of unending penance, my sole wish being I'd died along with my family or been locked up for wilful neglect.

Bringing me back to the present is the bell on the door, the one I can't get used to. Weary of jumping and turning each time it sounds, I am unable to stop myself and whip my head around for the hundredth time that morning. A shock wave shudders through me as I mentally register, despite his more care worn appearance, that I know the man standing there. With several long strides, Steve's large hand reaches out to catch the handle of the coffee pot as it releases from my absent grip and his other arm folds me into him as my knees buckle. As I fall, I can't help thinking seven years of disappearing, of moving from one place to the next, was too long and not long enough.

Supporting me, Steve half carries, half drags me out of the restaurant. As we pass old Ned, he reaches out a withered arm and tugs at my sleeve. "Don't go, please don't go. Don't leave me."

The familiar red truck is in the parking lot, the paint showing markings from thousands of stray rocks. His wife, Macy, leans on the front hood and Steve passes over my care to her as he returns the coffee pot into the restaurant.

"Emily, oh, Emily, we found you." Macy takes me into her arms, and I breath in her familiar scent of fresh baking and lemon cleaner.

Aware of the heavy crunch of Steve's cowboy boots returning, I whisper, "please get me out of here."

More stable on my own two feet, I move to the rear door of the truck as Macy says, "you might want to sit in the front."

Ignoring her, not wanting to delay for one second leaving the parking lot and my useless job behind, I open the door. Greeting me inside are a pair of large brown eyes in a pudgy face. Shoulder length, strawberry blond hair with thick curls embrace the boy's small head. He is buckled into a child's seat with a tray in front. Crayons litter the surface along with the seats and floor. A colouring book is in front of him and he holds a dark green crayon. Those large eyes size me up, dismiss me and return to his fierce colouring for a second before firing out a question.

"Wanna know the most dangous way to travel?" His words are articulate for his age, the question asked while keeping his gaze on the picture.

"Sure."

"On a shark."

A smile emerges, a strange sensation on my face, the muscles withered and shortened from lack of use. "Never thought of that one."

Here is an energy I could surround myself with, so I climb in beside him. Brown eyes catch my gaze as I pull the seatbelt around to click into place, "or a dragon," he adds.

His expression is dead serious, and I want to match his mood, not allow my smile to broaden likes it wants to. "Right," I respond, "definitely not the best way to go."

Satisfied, he returns to his book, switching from green to purple. Macy gets in the front and turns her head around, "my son, Marshall." He makes a small noise of disagreement and she adds, "he prefers to be called Marsh."

"Your son?" My voice is strangled, the question coming out with a high-pitched lilt. When I left their children were the same age as mine and I quickly do some mental arithmetic; surely, they must all be well on their way to adult lives by now.

"Our happy little surprise."

A crayon appears in my line of vision and I take it, me and the child lean down to the serious business of colouring. The picture on my side is a large elephant with some messy squiggles of red already across the face and trunk. Marsh is working on a tiger, which is a mixture of green and purple, the outline of its' shape obscured by the intense energy of his crayon.

While engaged in keeping my crayon inside the lines and remembering the simple task of putting colour to paper, I give directions to the rundown motel I've been staying at since I pulled into this rural Ontario town two months ago. In another month, maybe two, I was thinking of making a break for the coast, taking the slow route on secondary highways. My hope was the strong winds of the east coast, sure to arrive with the winter months, would blow away my overpowering grief, or, possibly, if I stood in the right spot, me.

My few belongings are thrown into a beat-up suitcase and tossed carelessly into my SUV. Closing the hatch, I pause for a moment with eyes closed, my hand still on the door to mentally prepare myself. Giving it up as a lost cause, knowing nothing will improve the encounter, I turn around and head toward the office for a final showdown with Noelle, the bitter woman who runs the place and takes out her unhappiness by judging others with harsh criticism.

While she attempts to appear nonchalant, as though she hadn't been watching everything outside for the past ten minutes, Noelle doesn't acknowledge my presence as I place the room key on the counter. A thick, ring-fingered hand reaches forward, squashing the key and dragging it until it drops into a drawer. Piggy eyes remain glued to the television on the wall as she says in her voice of gravel, "you've paid for the entire month, no refunds." Stringy, black hair falls loosely over her shoulders and her puckered face remains fixed away from me, "so, just ditching. Pulling out and leaving Candice high and dry after she was kind enough to hire you," a small huff, causing the jellied lines of her forehead to furrow and crease, "you're all the same."

Without being aware of it, Macy has followed me into the office and now pulls my arm, ushering me out of the tiny space filled with the noxious fumes of misery. In the parking lot, I stand beside my SUV helpless. I look toward the red truck and the back seat where Marsh sits. Not wanting to be on my own anymore, I need the company of those who know me and my past to ease the quick deflation caused by Noelle's barb.

The key fob is gently lifted out of my fingers while Macy says, "you ride in the truck with Steve, I'll follow."

Seven hours of driving, with only brief stops for gas and lunch, before we stop for the night. The entire time, I follow Marsh's lead, allowing him to dictate our every move. After colouring, we explore his sticker albums, which takes us on a journey through his bug obsession. Picture books are read, naps taken, apples eaten, innumerable juice boxes sucked down.

Images of my children flash unbidden on the inside of my eyelids, appearing each time I blink. While still painful, I am aware of a small marble of light growing in the corner of my heart as I'm being lectured with four-year-old logic on life, the universe and being on the road. My eldest, Steph, was a tomboy with short hair and a gruff attitude, often found in oversized coveralls and tinkering on one of the old cars in the shop. Liam would follow his father around night and day: riding in the tractor, herding cattle, learning the ways of the land. It is my youngest, Kyle, who I see the most. His dreamy expression, his fascination with my grandmother's piano, the delight of old Ethel Curry, the local music teacher, at his natural talent, and pure singing voice.

My future ended on a day at the end of summer much like today. By my command, each member of my family died in succession. A few potatoes for dinner was all I wanted. One child after another was sent outside to the root cellar. Irritation grew as each failed to return. Supper was delayed, the house in disarray, and, as always, there were too many chores and too little time. Not once did an inkling of the disaster striking down occur to me.

Speaking the final words ever said to Dave, my husband, I barked out as he was coming through the door, covered in dust and bone tired, "please go and find out what the hell game they're playing and tell them to get in here right this instant. They have homework to do and supper is late as it is."

He never came back either. All of them succumbed in that godforsaken cellar, the old vegetables from two years ago rotting in the corner, another task never accomplished, the toxic fumes building in the confined space, the vent plugged by a mouse nest. A year later, I was still on the farm, a ghost of a living person. My final act on the place was to take the tractor and cave in the cellar, that crumbling chamber of death. Leaving the tractor idling in the tall grass, not caring if a fire started, I stood staring at the house, the one that held every good memory of the lives I had destroyed.

Less than an hour later, my suitcase was packed and thrown into the SUV, along with an air mattress, sleeping bag, and pillow. The bathroom was my last stop, frantically rummaging through drawers and cupboards, afraid someone would show up and I'd be caught, forced to stay when all I wanted was to run. Every pill bottle I'd acquired in the past year was swept into a large grocery bag and dumped in the burn barrel on my way down the drive. Prescription induced release from my tormented thoughts was undeserved, I required all the punishment life could throw my way.

Many times I've lamented the things left behind. Nothing was safe while I was responsible for it, so pictures and keepsakes remained in the house. I'd not wanted to buy the SUV, had wished for another truck, but Dave thought it would be better as the children got older, more leg room and seating space. Giving in, it had come home two days before my family died, still smelling new with only a 157km on it. Not like the truck, which was littered with detritus from years of use: toys, odd pieces of clothing, hand smudges on the windows. Sometimes I sat in the truck, suspended in grief, but it had too much of my family in it and so I'd taken the SUV.

Driving away, spitting gravel in my need to go, I wondered for the thousandth time about my last mistake. Upon seeing my husband sprawled on the bottom step of the cellar entrance, his arms cradling the lifeless body of Kyle, I should have joined them, curled myself around their bodies and allowed the odourless gas to take my life as well. Instead, I'd raced for the house, grabbed the phone and called for help.

Talking to the nameless, faceless man at 9-1-1, who I still hated for his calm kindness, I melted into panic. Not released until the paramedics entered the house, that kind voice kept me glued to the phone, asking questions and keeping me talking, preventing me from returning to the scene of my crime.

Bringing me back to the present is a tug on my sleeve, and the insistent voice of Marsh, pointing out we've stopped, and demanding to be unbuckled. The hotel is a nice one, expensive, not the rundown holes I've been living in. Marsh is excited about everything, the empty swimming pool with a slide, the lobby and it's oversized plants and plush couches, the prospect of eating in a restaurant again.

Adjoining rooms with an interconnecting door are booked. Nobody can move fast enough for Marsh, who wants to be in the swimming pool, telling me he was a sea otter last year and failed so has to repeat it and he really wants to be a salamander so has to do lots of practicing. Talking so fast it is hard to keep up, he informs me that he can't become a salamander until he puts his face in the water, but he doesn't like it and doesn't know why he has to do it.

As soon as I am ready, I am rushed out of the room. Marsh runs as fast as his short legs can carry him and pushes the button for the elevator a hundred times until it finally arrives. Luckily, the pool is still empty, and we have it to ourselves for the first forty minutes while Macy sits in a lounger. I am content to be bossed around and not make any decisions, continuing to allow Marsh to lead the activities. Returning to the rooms, I shower under the hottest water my skin will tolerate, washing away sticky memories and the grime of seven years of running.

During dinner, Marsh fades into tiredness and Steve carries him upstairs. Sitting on my bed, alone again, I listen to the family sounds from beyond the connecting door and feel my loss descending again. A soft knock arrives on the door, which I didn't properly latch, and is pushed open. Marsh pads in with a book in hand, his pajamas covered in dancing teddy bears. Reaching up to be helped onto the bed, he snuggles in next to me, holding out his book and informing me I must read him a bedtime story. The marble in my heart grows as I turn the first page and start reading.

10 TEMPERING JOY

"How did your wife die?"

"Heating pad."

Said not as a warning but because it gives me a secret thrill, a glow inside, a tingle from my toes to the tips of my greying hair. My children believe the entire ordeal is tragic and are crushing me in cloying concern. All I feel is relief. A marriage I no longer wanted has conveniently dissolved with no effort on my part. Now I am cozily holed up in a hotel while my wife and house, the one I hated and never wanted to buy, are smoldering ruins.

Kaput. Out of my life for good. I pour another dram of ridiculously expensive cognac and toast my good fortune. During the day, it behooves me to behave as the responsible, grieving husband. At night, delight and pleasure sneak in, bubble up and make me giggle like a schoolgirl. Here, double bolted into my room, I am free to exercise excessive mirth.

Three meals a day, housekeeping while I'm not here, a large bed all to myself, and watching whatever I damn well please on the television. Not having to share a bathroom with multitudes of bottles and potions, long hair clogging the sink, or the lingering scent of a flowery perfume allows me to inhale my surroundings with pleasure. Nothing but heaven is what life has become. With insurance money covering costs, my expenditures each day are limited to tips and, quite frankly, I'm saving money.

If I'm honest, it is not the heating pad I should be grateful to, but the fall she took three days prior to her death. My wife, always in a hurry and super busy in her own importance, came storming out of the dentist with her mouth still swollen, head groggy from a sinus headache the night before, and thoughts focused on her next task. Not watching her footing, wearing the wrong shoes, her weak ankle rolled and down she went.

Did she call? No, not then, independent demon she was. Got up, hobbled down the remaining stairs to the sidewalk, limped to her car and drove home. Hours later, having prised her poor selection of footwear off, she was on the couch with an icepack and sent me a text. It was last Friday afternoon, the let's get to the weekend lethargy had fully settled in and everyone, myself included, was dragging themselves through the remainder of the day. Her message allowed me to gracefully leave the classroom early, to abandon ship and, silly me, look forward to a bit of relaxation leading into the weekend.

Having done her research, always prepared is my wife, she knew by late Sunday she needed to switch from ice to heat and I offered to get the heating pad for her. The thing is, trust was not the bedrock of our relationship. By every look and gesture, she informed me just how incompetent I was. So, with me following - a faithful trained mutt - she limped down the hallway towards the linen closet.

"Christ," she muttered, "you can't even find something that's right in front of your face, how are you going to locate a heating pad I haven't laid eyes on in over a year?"

Glaring at me over her shoulder, she advanced on the door with malice, hauling it open so hard the door, temperamental at the best of times, came off the tracking. This event caused the first deep sigh to come rushing out of her body. Another irritated look was directed my way before she ducked inside to rummage around. Within a few minutes, towels and sheets were being thrown out on the floor, the sighs now being emitted in rapid succession, the wayward door kicked for good measure.

Emerging from the closet, a noise of victory was emitted. Eyes bright with triumph, she held up the crumpled and folded heating pad as evidence of her superiority. Whatever my expression, it changed her tune quickly and her stare became disapproving once again.

"Why must you hover?"

"I'm not sure it would be wise to use that," pointing to the heating pad. In retrospect, my comment guarantees she can never accuse me, from whatever dimension she currently resides in, of not warning her. She'll try, I'm sure of it. It will torture her soul to see how happy I am at her demise.

"It will be fine." Hobbling back to the living room, she pushed me aside, "*please*...," the word was drawn out in exaggerated detail. "Get. Out. Of. My. Way." After a few more steps, she added with a dismissive flick of her fingers, "clean the mess up."

Disdain and contempt were my reward for unending loyalty, nothing more to her than a fetch and carry boy. My inability to predict her every wish and whim was the primary issue in our marriage. How she managed to marry such a doofus was beyond her, as she so often reminded me, arms flung in the air, words mumbled but intent clear.

By Sunday night, my office at the college beckoned. There were lessons to plan, and emails to check. Nothing urgent, all easily accomplished from home, but the thought of one more minute in my darling wife's company caused a tightening of the abdomen, my temples to throb and my fists to clench into fists. Drifting into a reverie, I could hear my shoes echoing down the empty corridor toward my tiny sanctuary, whispering with each step, "welcome back." The dim lighting reserved for evenings and weekends would highlight my path, calming me.

Ensconced on the couch with leg cushioned by blankets and pillows, my wife looked nothing less than cozy. Gently, I placed the remotes for the stereo and TV on the table beside her, and, for the third time in the space of ten minutes, I queried her level of comfort, and asked if she needed anything further. Making it clear I was being a nuisance, she picked up a book, and dismissed me with the crisp turn of a page.

Watching my tone, I attempted a gentle exit, "I need to get to the office and finish up some work for tomorrow morning." My weak and subservient voice caused me to wince, especially as the hint of a whine emerged at the edges. Inwardly, I reprimanded my feet, which bounced from one foot to the other allowing her to see the physical evidence of my discomfort, how much I wished to leave.

The face she turned to me was overcome with incredulousness, her mouth slightly open in disbelief, "really?" Even though she had no further use of me, I was expected to stand by at attention. Not in the same room - no, no, no - but close enough I would respond with utmost speed to her every whim.

"Yep." Not able to help myself, I repeated once again, "can I get you anything before I go? Are you comfortable?" Begging by this point, my hands itching to come together in prayer position, my dancing feet relentless. *Release me, release me, release me.*

Eyes returned to the page, words spat out, "whatever, do what you want. Lock the door on your way out."

Condescension mixed with forced apathy was her fallback response when displeased. My fidgeting stopped, my need to argue fought with walking out the door. I chose to leave. The fights were futile, nothing ever resolved, the same ground pounded over and over, identical bridges burned one more time. All of it useless.

At the college, safely locked inside my office, I sat and listened to the sound of nothing. Lights off, my chair kicked back and feet on the desk, tasks begging for my attention predictably remained untouched. After an hour, maybe it was two, I pulled my phone from my worn and battered briefcase, docked it and began a random shuffle of my favourite playlist, the one I labelled *Beautiful Music.*

Not an expert on music by any means, I am a dedicated voyeur to the whims and fancies of hosts on classical music programs. During a monthly purchasing spree, I attempt to decipher my scrawl on hastily written notes and my latest wishes are downloaded so *Beautiful Music* can be updated.

Compositions which touch a yearning deep within, one I am unable to articulate with words, is what I passively search for. I know it belongs on my playlist when the notes tremor along my spine and radiate outwards, engulfing my entire spirit. Even though I constantly add to the playlist, I have listened to it so often I can hum along at times, vocalize the odd note. Not well or in key, but it is done unintentionally and always gives me a secret thrill, an affirmation the piece is committed into my being and is now a part of me.

The night my house went up in flames, my Bose docking station created a shower of sound, bathing me in serenity. The thought of returning home nudged briefly at my brain, but I remained where I was, ass going numb from sitting too long in my office chair. By the time I left, it was hours too late. Our house was ashes on the ground, her body crispy bacon.

Not a single tinge of regret echoes within me as I play out memories best left alone. Finishing the last mouthful of cognac, I lean against the cushioned headboard, savouring the comfort of a thick mattress. My right arm extends to full length, reaching for a few more cubes of ice from the bucket on the floor. A little oops as I almost fall and another giggle of pure glee escapes. Righting myself, I throw the ice in my glass and grab the bottle tucked behind the lamp on the bedside table.

Pouring a smidge more, I hold the glass up and decide to fill it, no use tinkering around. Embracing the excuse of tonight's drinking being therapeutic is how I rationalize it, repeating out loud how I need to fortify myself, and the serious business of getting drunk is well deserved. The funeral, that endless parade of unwanted sympathy, is set for tomorrow. There is no escaping it, I am required. It is vital I show support for our children, to receive from those assembled in turn.

The next morning is as bad as predicted, not helped by my hangover. Upon waking, four Tylenol were rattled into my shaking palm, mouth held under the tap of the bathroom sink to wash them down. Needless to say, the pills are doing little to hold back the pain of my pounding head. Unaccountably, the sky is an endless blue with the sun shining cruelly bright, and my cheap sunglasses afford inadequate protection. I make a resolution, as the casket is lowered into the ground, to buy a good pair of shades tomorrow, one with a price tag to cause shortness of breath, maybe even polarized lenses. It's refreshing to know I can make these selfish decisions without fear of scrutiny or having to explain myself.

With son on one side and daughter on the other, both leaning into me to support and be supported, the minister drones on. Sunglasses added to my lengthening mental shopping list; I fantasize about the condo I will buy. A condo will be perfect. I never want to shovel another sidewalk or mow the grass again. I'd rather sit on my balcony and watch whatever schmucks the board hires do it, toasting them with my drink of the day for their diligence.

My face must be a mask of pain as I try to hold in laughter threatening to engulf me. A small tear leaks out of the corner of my eye, blissfully mistaken as a sign of sadness. I feel the relentless grip of my daughter, the spitting image of her mother – god help her – tighten to a blood constricting clutch. The woman being lowered into the ground, well-read bitch she was, would say I was behaving in an unctuous manner. Ah well, her meagre degree in humanities, her lording it over me, wielding her blade of superiority, is no longer a part of my life. Breaking away from my support network, I burst through the crowd. Running clumsily away, I search for cover. It is imperative I go far enough not to be heard, and finally collapse against a weathered headstone to succumb, briefly and privately, to my elation.

Several minutes later, under control again, I begin to saunter back to reside at the helm of mourners. My steps are slow, small, and reluctant. With many pauses, pretending to meditate on grave marker messages, I regard the crowd around my wife's freshly dug plot, and decide to join them when it is obvious the service is over.

Another aspect of the plan I've been contemplating is not returning to work anytime soon. Using up all my compassionate leave, extending it with my banked vacation days and, maybe, adding on some long-term stress leave. Given the circumstances, all of it would be completely reasonable. It is fitting all those vacation days my wife made me save, all the over-time I had to take so we could properly enjoy our retirement, will now be mine to do with as I wish.

Tomorrow, I will insist my son and daughter return home to their families. Homes that are blissfully so far away it takes planning or tragedy to bring them to my side. Working to my advantage will be my supposed grief. I will beg off phone calls for the next while, insist email is my preferred method of communication. As the clincher, I'll tell them writing allows me time and space to compose my thoughts adequately. They'll understand, my daughter simpering platitudes of nothing, my son as incapable as I've always been of uttering the right words.

Working this wedge of my deceit will allow me to fly to a tropical paradise. Whiling away long hours on the beach, sitting under an umbrella with a bar nearby offering chair service is the first vital step forward. I will shed off the persona of the fuddy duddy, a seasoned grandpa snuggling into a slow decline. Carefree and lighthearted, my sights set on retirement, my fingers will be busy recalculating how much further our savings will go with only me to spend it any way I please.

13 Ways to Die

11 SUMMER FREEZES

Summer closes the car door and stumbles up the hill, wondering how far she needs to go before getting a signal. Her feet and bare legs wade through thick snow, which absorb her panic. Within steps it has become a slog, her white runners not able to give traction and she goes down several times, the shrubs and other hibernating plant life etching memories in her knees and legs. The short skirt she's wearing gives her little cover, and she pulls it back down a few times before giving up. Who is out here to see?

The accident occurred without warning when she and Mitch were discussing some idle gossip from school. She was looking out the window at the dark night when the car jolted, and Mitch lost control. After a few fishtails, the car slipped off the road, careening down a steep bank and coming to an abrupt halt just before the partially frozen creek. Silence engulfed the car for several moments before they were able to ascertain that, apart from a few bumps and bruises, both seemed to be okay.

The car stalled on impact. When Mitch tried to restart it, that old engine fired up immediately and with an expression of relief he jumped out to check for damage, using his cell phone as a flashlight. Soon afterwards, he ran up the hill, using the last of his battery to call that moron Ryan. Mitch stayed up on the road hoping to flag someone down for help. It was a rural, gravel road and, on this night, deserted. In his jeans and thin shirt, he was soaked through and shivering by the time he returned to the car. Ryan promised he would be there soon, so Mitch was still upbeat: the car was running, the damage looked minimal and, at that point, it looked as though they still might make the party.

The snow continued to fall, and the temperature continued to drop. With wet clothes, it was lethal. Since the old car only put out a feeble amount of heat, Summer urged Mitch to take his off. Mitch had taken this to mean that he and Summer were finally going to have sex, which had annoyed her, so they stopped speaking, each trapped in their own private misery. When the car ran out of gas an hour ago, Mitch wasn't doing very well, his speech was already slurred and his movements uncoordinated. Nonetheless, he jumped out of the car to retrieve an old, oil stained rug from the trunk to help keep Summer warm, his peace offering.

Soon afterward, Summer finally managed to cajole him into removing his wet, partially frozen clothing and climb into the backseat. By that time, Mitch was nodding off and unable to hold a coherent conversation, so Summer did most of the work herself. She found some dirty clothes lying on the floor and used those to cover him up, placing the rug on top. The effort had restored some warmth into her body and forced her to acknowledge that it was almost too late, they were both going to die in that car unless she made the call. Not wanting to end up like Mitch, she chose not to curl up beside him. Instead, she carefully removed her socks and both pairs of stockings, so she would have something warm and dry to put back on when she returned.

By the time Summer scrambled up the hill, they had been in the ditch for hours. Ryan was never going to show up, had probably been too drunk to drive when Mitch called him and, as far as Summer could tell, was useless at the best of times. Her father will be furious over the lack of essentials: no winter tires, no emergency kit, no common sense, no nothing. Only her lies and stupidity in defiance of her parents for refusing to give her permission to go, saying it was irresponsible to go all the way out to hell and gone for some high school party, particularly in winter. Mitch was going to the party with or without her and Summer wanted so much to go. Now all her reasonings seem feeble, and she can't remember why it felt important. In the pitch black, attempting to navigate the hill, she can clearly see her father sitting at the kitchen table earlier that afternoon.

"There is a no travel advisory out for tonight, Buttercup."

Rolling her eyes, Summer continued to pull on her boots, "I'm only going two blocks over to Cheryl's house Dad."

Indeed, Summer had gone over to Cheryl's house, just long enough to change her clothes into those she was wearing to the party. When Mitch picked her up, the three of them had laughed about her deviousness, like it was all a big joke. Wasn't a joke now. Mitch, the dummy, had left the city with insufficient fuel and no money, which Summer hadn't known about until the car ran out of gas, thinking, like a child, the car would last the night and everything would still be okay.

Pulling her phone out of the waistband of her skirt, where her body heat had kept it warm, she touches the screen to check her battery is still good, sighing with relief that it still holds more than a 50% charge. The signal shows only one bar and she hopes it is enough to make the call. Her hands are numb and shaking but, she manages to push the right contact and hold the phone to her ear. Like he's been waiting all night for the call, he answers before the first ring ends.

"Summer?"

Summer starts to cry at the sound of his voice, "Daddy."

"Where are you honey?"

"Don't know."

"Can you turn your GPS back on?"

Summer forgot she'd turned it off, another element of her little plan, and reluctantly pulls the phone away from her ear. Frozen fingers fumble with the phone and she pushes icons she doesn't want, causing her to cry harder and become more incompetent. After what feels like forever, she finally gets the GPS back on and places the phone back to her ear.

Her father doesn't wait for her voice, "okay, I got it. I'm on my way." She can hear the slam of his truck door, the start of the engine.

"Summer, sweetie, are the hazard lights on the car blinking."

"No."

"Can you turn them on?"

"No."

A brief pause, "are you in the car now?"

"No, no signal."

A sigh, "okay Sweetie. Go back to the car and turn the hazard lights on? Stay with the car and try to dial 9-1-1 from there. Don't leave the car again. Got it?"

"Yes," her voice is small and shaky, she wonders if any sound came out at all.

"Good. I need you to hang up now. I am on my way, I promise Buttercup."

Hanging up only because he asked her to and not because she wants to, she tucks the phone back into her waistband, maybe the only warm spot left on her body, and starts to stumble and fall back down the hill. When she gets there, she pushes her shoes off, leaving them outside in the snow. The first thing she does is reach over to push on the hazard lights, stretching her body across the front seat, one of her bare legs extending out through the open passenger door. After closing the door, she sits on the seat for a moment, her knees pulled up into her chest, hands holding her feet and rocks back and forth. She needs to get herself together, get out of her wet clothes, then dial 9-1-1. Summer continues rocking, the rhythm is comforting, and she starts humming a soothing lullaby from her childhood.

The crinkling of her skirt as it starts to freeze finally calls Summer back into action. With movements that are slow and uncoordinated, she pulls off her wet skirt and underwear and throws them on the floor before reaching over to grabs her thin, inside tights. She has trouble getting them on because her legs are still wet and starts crying again, which causes her to lose what little vision the darkness allows. Her hands are shaking and not working properly, and the tights are twisted and uncomfortable by the time she finally gets them on. Even so, they feel good, a little barrier between her and the cold.

It takes another several minutes to work up the energy to grab the thicker, wool tights and start pulling them over top of the thin ones. The inside ones are such a mess that the wool ones won't go up all the way. She thinks she might have them on the wrong way, but once she has struggled to get them up as high as she can, she can't be bothered to take them off again and get it right.

Her fingers feel like frozen claws, and she quickly pulls her thick socks on and resumes her position of knees to chest, her hands tucked up inside her coat next to her body. Slow rocking and humming of the lullaby recommence, Summer no longer able to remember all the words but content to repeat the same verse over and over. She knows she should try to call 9-1-1 and then climb into the backseat, get under that gross rug with Mitch, see if he still has a pulse. She knows she should keep him warm, but all she can do is rock – back and forth, side to side, back and forth, side to side.

The opening of the passenger car door jolts her awake. Before she is fully conscious, two large arms reach in and haul her out, folding her into a thick, warm blanket.

"Hey Summer girl, I got you."

Not her father, not yet. She knows he'll be here; knows with the sound of Chet's voice that he has put his wide-reaching network into effect. Chet takes long, quick strides up the hill, heading toward a truck idling on the side of the road with headlights shining through the dark. When they arrive, he pulls open the rear door and carefully places her inside.

"Be right back, Sylvie will take care of you."

A hand rests on her shoulder, which Summer ignores as she watches Chet's large frame disappear into the swirling snow, which is still falling thick and heavy. He carefully maneuvers down the embankment, his body resembling a moving shadow for a few moments before disappearing into the night. The hazards on Mitch's car are barely visible, the lights blinking slowly, draining the last power from the car's battery. Waiting, Summer watches those lights intently, becoming lost in their hypnotizing slowness. Chet finally appears again holding Mitch's lifeless body just as the ambulance pulls over in front of the truck. No sirens, just the swirling red and blue lights that cause a kaleidoscope effect with the falling snow.

The warm hand on her shoulder gives a gentle squeeze and Sylvie speaks, "hey, Summer, honey."

Summer allows herself to collapse into Sylvie's body, curling herself up as small as possible into a life changed forever.

Samantha Johnson

12 VIGILANTE

Those poor boys, all lined up neatly in a row, six feet of dirt covering them. They are all similar to the one I will dispose of tonight. My preferred practice is to let each of them know it is I, slip of a thing, who killed them, I who will bury them, and I who owns the secret. Not all are as well researched as my current target, but each are justifiably dead. Men must pay the price for centuries of degradation. Let's be reasonable, being men, their crimes will be many and varied. There is no need for judge and jury, only quick justice.

This one is a cop, and I will need to be careful tonight. His wife never leaves the house without dark sunglasses, long sleeved shirts and a turtleneck, no matter the heat outside. On my last visit I saw her through a crack in the curtains, hair matted with blood, three small children cowering around her while my potential victim screamed with rage. Objects thrown, house torn asunder, glass showering the room with each delicate item he touched, the cupboards emptied of plates and glasses. It is all her fault, that is what he will tell her, and then make her pay for it again and again.

With my possessions is a folder of glossy photos. To it will be added those I will take tonight - of the grave and his dead body - before mailing it to his colleagues. In each of my assignments, I leave the wives out of the picture, not wanting them to be fingered for the deed. The collection contains evidence of his cheating ways, how he beats his wife, the illegal sidekicks he gets as part of his job. Ensuring she has an alibi, I will order a pizza to her house, prepaid, just before I make contact with her soon to be deceased husband.

The target has no less than three mistresses, each one younger than the last. All have naivety dripping from fresh faces, the inward curve of their lower spine a telling sign of innocence. Each was initially flattered by his overbearing attention, his uniform and the assumed protection it afforded.

Now they remain available out of fear, lacking the expertise and knowledge on how to disappear and make a timely escape. An intensely jealous man, he warns them of the dangers of infidelity while he knocks on each of their doors with lipstick on his collar, the scent of perfume drenching his clothing. Aside from his mistresses, he enjoys a steady stream of one-night stands, the odd hooker at a reduced rate.

Sex in public places is one of his vices. Empty parking lots, deserted streets, beside dumpsters in alleys with rotting smells assaulting the senses of his latest conquest. Places where they could be caught but it's unlikely to happen. Jeopardizing his reputation on the force is not on his agenda. Degrading the young pieces of fluff his primary objective and he excels at it, pushing their bare asses against windows, exhibiting them spread eagled on the hood of his truck, or bent over at the waist with hands holding onto a railing outside a subway station or someone's house. He is rough with them, scratching, biting and pinching, ramming into them until they bleed, demanding, all the while, they yell to the world how much they adore him as he hurts them.

Playing hard to get has been my ploy for the cop, who I've been tracking for over a year. When I left last time, he was practically frothing at the mouth. Tonight, I wear the outfit of the catholic schoolgirl, saddle shoes and all, my mouth a pout of red lipstick, my hair straight with one side clipped back in a red barrette. My course in theatre makeup, which I took in my younger, more hopeful days, comes in handy to mask my features, hide small wrinkles around my eyes and mouth.

Ripe for new blood, bored with the predictability of submission by each of his mistresses, I make myself an obvious choice. Entering the dark bar in a low-down part of the city, I am an instant sensation. Recognizing me, he moves in as protection as I glide down the bar, lustful eyes on all sides greedily watching.

Ignoring him, I accept the offer of a drink from another patron. Pot belly hangs over his stool and the desperate man probably hasn't seen his dick in years, only knows it's still there from feel alone. I become an outrageous flirt, dropping my lipstick and jumping off the stool, bending over as I feel my short skirt rise up to the bottom of my buttocks, smiling at the collective intake of breath. Flouncing down the bar, I sit on knees, allow excessive groping, bringing my target's jealousy to a steaming froth.

Prancing back to collect my discarded drink and give my patron a little rub on the arm, to see if he still responds, cop man grabs my arm, "enough of the coquette, you and I are leaving." Pulling me out the door, he pushes me up against his jacked-up diesel truck. "I could fuck you right here, you've played with me for too long."

Mauling me, hands all over my body in his frenzy of lust, I am able to frisk him – no gun tonight - as I fake appropriate attraction. Making small noises of protest, I beg for my virtue and respectability.

"No woman who enters a place like that dressed as you are has any respect, you deserve what I am going to give you."

My arms reach around his neck and he lifts me off the ground, my back sliding up the side of the truck. Interested only in nuzzling my breasts and putting his fingers inside me, the blade in my long, thick socks is not noticed. Nibbling on his ear, making him groan, I whisper, "we have a crowd."

He jerks his head around to take in the motley crew gathering at the door of the bar, the men practically salivating at the sight of me, clothes in disarray, skirt hiked up to display my lacy underwear. Fingers and hands are removed, and my dress is roughly pulled down.

"Back inside boys, no show here." Flashing his badge and inching keys out of the front pocket of his jeans, he clicks the lock open and pushes me into the passenger seat. Giving the men a wolfish grin, he trots around the front hood to get into the driver's seat. The truck starts with a low rumble of power he pauses to savour, a joy that never grows old for him, before placing it in gear and roaring off down the street.

After a few minutes, all innocence and virginal naivety, I say, "how about the old Brandon farmhouse, I hear it's haunted."

A hard right is taken, altering direction, my seatbelt holding me as I'm thrown against the door. Silence fills the cab, the large console between the seats preventing physical contact. I am tantalizingly close yet out of reach. Hunched over the steering wheel, he avoids turning my way, keeping both eyes focused on the road, wanting to reach our destination as soon as possible. His thoughts are easy to read, no skill required. Mine are an iron fist, focused on specifics and drawing out a map of my plan for the night.

Once business is complete, I will hit the road. I never hire a car when visiting, relying on public transit and walking. Unwise to fling my name around unnecessarily, booking and paying for my accommodation and food with prepaid, untraceable credit cards. A reliable contact a few hours drive west will take the truck off my hands, and have it dismantled by morning. Hard cash in hand, I will change disguises, jump on a train and travel further west.

A hankering for the coast has been itching my insides for months. Maybe Portland is a smart place to start, hopping onto a ferry bound for Vancouver Island, renting a car once back in my home country. From there, cruising home can be done at super slow speed. I've moved quickly, only three days into my vacation and ten left to go, lots of time to take it easy.

Our destination in sight, he takes the corner too fast and barrels down the dark drive. As he pulls up hard in front of the old house, I jump out and skip, giggling onto the porch. The faded green and white frame lists to one side after years of being battered by the elements, the front door lying useless in the front yard. I know this house like the back of my hand and run inside, pretending to hide. Caught in the kitchen, as per my plan, the husks of long dead mice litter the corners, broken glass crunching underfoot, the few remaining cupboard doors swinging on rusty hinges.

He picks me up and places my ass on the edge of the dirty counter, covers my mouth with his. There is an edge of desperation to his groping now, a man who has waited too long for his hard-earned prize. Submission is key, gives them a taste of what they think is to come, make them believe I want it as much as they do.

Tongue in his ear, swirling it in a circle, "let's try the barn," I say, "it's so dirty here."

Because I am a novelty, he agrees. With a grunt, he carries me out the back door, the barn doors rattling in anticipation even though the night has not a speck of wind. Inside he lays me out on fresh straw I laid down yesterday, kneels and starts unbuckling his jeans. I push him onto his back with my small, dainty hand and straddle him, inching upwards until I am sitting on his face.

Panties so loose and frayed, as well as cut strategically with scissors before I left for the evening, it takes one brisk tug for them to be ripped and gone, flung into the reaches of the barn. A model citizen, my DNA will mean nothing to the investigating officers. His mouth searches for me eagerly, taking the bait, my skirt a blanket over his head. Noises of pleasure are forced from my throat as my arm reaches back and my fingers ease out the knife.

"More, more," I screech to the rotting wooden walls. The game is over now, I have won, and I raise the knife high, marvelling at the beauty of the sharp blade. It glints in the shaft of moonlight penetrating through a hole in the roof and I smile at my success. With a well-practiced move, I gracefully lift my body off him and bring the knife down to pierce his neck. One, two, three times.

13 RELEASE

Turning off the path, I follow a dirt trail, my need to be alongside the river strong. The trail narrows, then disappears. Rather than turn back, I continue forward, crashing through the trees toward the rushing sound of moving water. A pouch of pelicans lounging on the submerged bank are spooked by my approach. This chance sighting provides a twinkling of beauty before my world comes crashing down. I become lost in the magnificence of their large, black-tipped white wings moving in a slow, deep rhythm. Orange bills contrast against the sky, flashing in and out of the tree cover as they fly overhead. Standing perfectly still, I tilt my neck back to watch them. While I am distracted, my hearing attuned to wing flights on the air, he comes thundering towards me and makes his attack.

Caught unaware, I briefly disconnect from myself, remaining with the pelicans in flight as he slams my body into the ground. My head strikes a large rock, and I stare dazed up at a large tree and wish myself enfolded into it, awaking into an Entish dream. Uniting with the ground and becoming one with the roots, my vascular system a conduit for nutrients and bones a structured web of strength, is preferable to the reality I need to face.

The earth delivers her song through the rustle of leaves and whispering of insects, and I return into myself. The weight of his body covers me, and his wet, fetid breath is hot against my neck. Revulsion churns in my stomach, allowing me to choke back fear and find my rage, to await my moment. One of his large hands holds both of mine above my head, and his other is grasping at zippers and buttons; ripping and tearing, he shreds clothing off me, preparing an opening for his release.

I know his face. He has been pursuing me for months and I have been fending him off. Mildly at first, later more forcefully. During the past month, I saw his decrepit white car, with a little dark green tree of poison swinging from the rear-view mirror, parked on the block outside my apartment building. Today it was absent, and I thought myself safe for this ramble. In the past weeks, I have been searching for new jobs, apartment hunting but knew I would have to change cities to rid myself of him with no guarantee of success. He has become a tick that holds on, irritating and not leaving, driving an infection deep within. My rejection has brought out a mean streak, and he punches and kicks me, spitting his hateful words in my ear. I am not the one who is allowed to refuse him: he will own me. I will pay. I will submit.

Thinking my fight is over, and I have yielded, he lifts slightly off me, allowing me the moment I've been waiting for. He continues to hold my hands, using the other to liberate his engorged anger caught within his too tight jeans. Finding strength, I heave my body with force to claw, twist, and scream my resistance. It is enough to loosen his grip, a microsecond of chance. I pound and struggle my way from that soul deathbed in the mud onto my knees and, as I am rising to stand, a new attack begins. His fury is acute and obscenities harsh as I kick back, my boot contacting his chin.

Rising up, my feet find solid ground and I stagger into a run, heading towards the most reliable source of rescue available. The river is swollen with spring rain and mountain snowmelt: running high, fast, and muddy. It is a suicidal torrent, a swirling mass of flowing death. I run straight into the water, which reaches past my knees in a few steps. Turning back toward the riverbank, my body quakes in the rough current. It is a standoff neither can win. He takes a step closer and holds out his hand, greed and lust still evident, his offer as my saviour insincere. The cold attacks my bones, and I wait no longer. I kneel into the water to release myself, allowing the river to wash me clean away.

ABOUT THE AUTHOR

Samantha Johnson lives in Medicine Hat, Alberta with too many animals. She does freelance work with a weekly paper and works on creative projects whenever she can. Yoga, cooking and gardening take up large portions of her time.

Manufactured by Amazon.ca
Bolton, ON

33644490R00046